TALES FROM THE
MAYAN DIVINE

by Samuel DenHartog

Published by STUDIOS SINALOA

1st Edition. 2024.

Table of Contents

[CHAPTER 1] — ACAT 4

[CHAPTER 2] — AH CILIZ 7

[CHAPTER 3] — AH HULNEB 10

[CHAPTER 4] — AH MUZEN CAB 15

[CHAPTER 5] — AH PUCH 18

[CHAPTER 6] — AH TZUL 22

[CHAPTER 7] — AHAU CHAMAHEZ 26

[CHAPTER 8] — AHAU KIN 30

[CHAPTER 9] — AJBIT 33

[CHAPTER 10] — AWILIX...37

[CHAPTER 11] — BACABS 40

[CHAPTER 12] — BITOL 43

[CHAPTER 13] — BOLON TZACAB 46

[CHAPTER 14] — CAMAZOTZ...49

[CHAPTER 15] — CHAAC...53

[CHAPTER 16] — CHIN 56

[CHAPTER 17] — CHITAM...59

[CHAPTER 18] — CIZIN...63

[CHAPTER 19] — CIT BOLOM TUM...............................66

[CHAPTER 20] — COLEL CAB 69

[CHAPTER 21] — EK CHUAH...72

[CHAPTER 22] — HUNAB KU 76

[CHAPTER 23] — HUN-HUNAHPU AND VUCUB-
HUNAHPU 79

[CHAPTER 24] — ITZAMNA 82

[CHAPTER 25] — IXCHEL 87

[CHAPTER 26] — IXMUCANÉ AND IXPIYACOC 90

[CHAPTER 27] — IXTAB 97

[CHAPTER 28] — IXCHUP 100

[CHAPTER 29] — IX TUB TUN 105

[CHAPTER 30] — IXQUIC 108

[CHAPTER 31] — JACAWITZ 111

[CHAPTER 32] — JURAKAN 114

[CHAPTER 33] — KINICH AHAU 117

[CHAPTER 34] — KINICH KAKMO 121

[CHAPTER 35] — KUKULKAN 124

[CHAPTER 36] — MAM 127

[CHAPTER 37] — NACON 131

[CHAPTER 38] — PAWAHTUN 134

[CHAPTER 39] — TOHIL 137

[CHAPTER 40] — WAYEB 140

[CHAPTER 41] — VUCUB CAQUIX 144

[CHAPTER 42] — XAMAN EK 147

[CHAPTER 43] — XBALANQUE AND HUNAHPÚ 150

[CHAPTER 44] — YALUK 160

[CHAPTER 45] — YUM KAAX 164

[CHAPTER 46] — YUMIL KAXOB 167

[CHAPTER 47] — ZIPACNA 170

[CHAPTER 48] — ZOTZ 173

ABOUT THE AUTHOR 179

[CHAPTER 1] — ACAT

Under the dense canopy of a jungle near Tikal, where the chatter of wildlife fills the air like a constant hum, lived a young tattoo artist named Xanil. His skill with the needle was unmatched, his designs imbued with such depth and detail that they seemed to dance on the skin. Yet, Xanil yearned for more; he sought to create art that transcended beauty, art that could weave the very essence of a person into their skin.

One evening, as the sun dipped below the horizon, painting the sky with hues of fire, Xanil ventured deeper into the jungle than he had ever dared. He whispered his desire to the ancient trees, hoping the spirits of the land might hear his plea. As night enveloped the world, a figure emerged from the shadows, adorned with intricate tattoos that glowed with an ethereal light. This was Acat, the deity of tattoos and body modification, whose presence commanded both awe and reverence.

Acat's voice, deep and resonant, broke the silence. "Xanil, your desire has echoed through the roots and vines of my domain. You seek to create art that binds the soul, a quest that few dare to dream." His tattoos shimmered with each word, captivating Xanil's gaze.

Xanil, though trembling, found the courage to speak. "Great Acat, teach me to imbue my art with the essence of life itself, so that my creations may reflect the depth of the soul."

Acat studied Xanil with eyes that held the wisdom of the ages. "To wield such power, you must understand the weight of your request. Your art will reveal truths, some of which might have been better left hidden. Are you prepared for such responsibility?"

Without hesitation, Xanil nodded, his determination clear.

Thus began Xanil's apprenticeship under Acat. Each night, under the canopy of stars, Acat taught Xanil the sacred art of tattoos that could bind a person's essence to their skin. He learned to mix inks from the jungle's heart, using herbs and minerals that held the jungle's spirit. He learned chants and rituals that invoked the energy of the earth, infusing each tattoo with power beyond mere decoration.

Months passed, and Xanil's art transformed. Those who came to him left with tattoos that were alive with the stories of their souls. A warrior from Uxmal bore a jaguar on his arm that seemed to move with his own strength and agility. A priestess from Palenque received an intricate feathered serpent that coiled around her wrist, its eyes gleaming with divine wisdom.

But with great power came consequences. A noble from Copán sought a tattoo that would reveal his true nature. What emerged was a design that writhed and shifted, a mirror to his deceit and ambition. The noble was horrified, for his inner darkness was laid bare for all to see.

Xanil realized the truth in Acat's warning. His art did not just embellish; it exposed the soul's deepest corners, bringing both awe and fear.

Acat, watching from the shadows, knew his pupil had understood the gift's complexity. "Your art will forever change those it touches, Xanil. Let it be a reminder of the power of truth and the weight of revealing it."

As Acat vanished into the night, leaving no trace but the glow of his tattoos lingering in the air, Xanil returned to his village, a changed man. His work continued to inspire and intimidate, a testament to the god who had shown him the soul's true canvas.

[CHAPTER 2] — AH CILIZ

Shadows crept across the vast plazas of Palenque, heralding an event rare and divine. It was a day like no other, when the sun, in its fiery chariot, would be devoured by the unseen beast of the cosmos. Nahil, a priestess devoted to the study of celestial movements, had predicted this day, her calculations etched meticulously on parchment, her mind a whirlwind of anticipation and reverence.

As the people of Palenque gathered, their eyes cast upwards, a chilling silence fell over the city. Nahil stood at the heart of the observatory, her gaze fixed on the sky, awaiting the moment when day would turn to night, when Ah Ciliz would reign supreme over the sun.

As the eclipse began, its shadow swallowing the light, a figure emerged from the darkness at the edge of the city. Cloaked in the ephemeral veil between day and night, Ah Ciliz moved with the grace of a being not bound by earthly tethers. His eyes, dark as the void, held the mysteries of the universe, and his voice, when it broke the silence, carried the weight of eons.

"Nahil, seeker of the heavens," he spoke, his voice a whisper on the wind, "you have called me forth, your devotion a beacon in the darkness. What is it you seek in the shadow of my embrace?"

Nahil, unflinching before the god of eclipses, responded with a voice steady and clear. "Great Ah Ciliz, I seek understanding. Show me the secrets that lie hidden in the darkness, the truths that only you can reveal."

Ah Ciliz regarded Nahil, a flicker of approval in his gaze. With a gesture, the world around them shifted, and together they ascended, spirits unbound, soaring into the heavens. Nahil witnessed the cosmic dance from a perspective few mortals ever could, the sun and moon in their eternal chase, the delicate balance of light and shadow.

As they returned to the earthly realm, the eclipse reaching its zenith, Ah Ciliz bestowed upon Nahil a gift—a pendant wrought from the heart of a star, its glow a mimicry of the corona seen around the sun during an eclipse. "Carry this," he intoned, "as a reminder that knowledge is found not in the light alone but in the embrace of darkness."

With those words, Ah Ciliz vanished, leaving Nahil alone as the light began to pierce the shadow once more. The people of Palenque, awestruck by the spectacle, found their priestess transformed, her eyes alight with the wisdom of the gods.

Nahil's experience with Ah Ciliz became a part of her, a silent knowledge that guided her in her duties, a reminder of the balance between light and dark. And though she never spoke of her journey among the stars, the pendant she wore became a symbol of her connection to the divine, a beacon of hope in the ever-turning cycle of life, death, and rebirth.

[CHAPTER 3] — AH HULNEB

Amidst the verdant cloak of the jungle that enshrouds Calakmul, whispers of unrest stirred the air, carrying the scent of impending turmoil far beyond the city's stately stone structures and towering pyramids. It was a time of unease, where the balance of power teetered on the brink of war. Two great Mayan cities, Calakmul and its long-standing rival, Tikal, stood at the precipice of conflict, fueled by disputes over territories and resources. At the heart of this brewing storm was K'an Joy Chitam, a young noble of Calakmul, whose destiny was about to intertwine with the divine.

As the tension escalated, K'an Joy Chitam sought counsel from the esteemed priests, who, under the cover of night, performed rituals to invoke guidance from the gods. Amidst the flickering flames and rising smoke, a presence formidable and awe-inspiring materialized before them — Ah Hulneb, the god of war, clad in armor that shimmered with the hues of blood and fire. His eyes, piercing as the obsidian blade, surveyed those gathered with an intensity that silenced the night.

"K'an Joy Chitam," Ah Hulneb's voice thundered, echoing through the temple's ancient halls, "you stand before me seeking victory, yet what have you offered in return?"

Humbled yet courageous, K'an Joy Chitam replied, "Great Ah Hulneb, we offer our valor and pledge the glory of our conquest to your name. Grant us your favor, and we shall vanquish our foes, securing Calakmul's might for generations to come. I will sacrifice a hundred of my greatest warriors to your name."

Ah Hulneb, unmoved by promises of glory and sacrifice, decreed a trial of unparalleled challenge. "Valor alone does not sway the course of war. You, K'an Joy Chitam, must embark alone upon a quest to the sacred cenote of Chichen Itzá. There, you shall retrieve the Obsidian Scepter, a relic of my power. Only then will you earn my favor."

K'an Joy Chitam's journey began as the first light of dawn crept over the horizon of Calakmul, bathing the ancient city in a golden hue. The air was heavy with anticipation, and the young noble's heart beat with a rhythm that echoed the war drums of his ancestors. The path before him was fraught with dangers untold, but the fire of determination burned within him, igniting a resolve as unyielding as the stone temples that towered above.

His first challenge emerged in the dense heart of the jungle, where the air thrummed with the life of a thousand creatures unseen. Here, K'an Joy Chitam faced the jaguar, its eyes glinting like emeralds in the shadowy underbrush. The beast, a guardian of the path, tested his courage and his strength. With a combination of agility and respect for the creature before him, K'an Joy Chitam passed the test, understanding that true strength lay in harmony with the natural world.

Further along the treacherous path, the young noble encountered a chasm as dark and daunting as the void. The only way across was a bridge, fragile and worn by time, suspended over the abyss. With each cautious step, K'an Joy Chitam felt the specter of failure looming over him, threatening to swallow him whole. Yet, it was here, in the face of his own fears and doubts, that he learned the value of faith — faith in himself and in the guidance of the gods.

At last, the sacred cenote lay before him, a gateway to the divine, its waters still and deep. As K'an Joy Chitam plunged into the cenote's depths, the chill of the water seeped into his bones, and visions of wars past enveloped him. Scenes of battle, of sacrifice and loss, unfolded before his eyes, each one a testament to the true cost of war. The cries of the fallen whispered in the dark waters, and K'an Joy Chitam felt the weight of their suffering pressing down upon him.

When his fingers finally closed around the Obsidian Scepter, a surge of understanding coursed through him. The scepter was not merely a symbol of power but a reminder of the responsibility that came with it — the duty to wield that power with wisdom and compassion. The burden of war, he realized, was a legacy of pain, a cycle of loss that left deep scars upon the land and its people.

Emerging from the cenote, K'an Joy Chitam was not the same young noble who had embarked on this quest. He carried with him the lessons of the jungle, the chasm, and the sacred waters — lessons of courage, faith, and the true cost of conflict.

Upon his return to Calakmul, the city received him with reverence, his journey having become a part of its storied history. When Ah Hulneb appeared to accept the Obsidian Scepter, the god of war stood before K'an Joy Chitam not as a figure of terror, but as a mentor, his presence a solemn reminder of the lessons learned.

In a voice that resonated with the depth of centuries, Ah Hulneb spoke, "K'an Joy Chitam, you have faced the darkness and emerged enlightened. Carry forth this knowledge, and let it guide you in the stewardship of your people. Let the wars of the past not be a path to the future but a memory from which to learn."

As Ah Hulneb vanished, leaving behind a silence filled with promise and peril, K'an Joy Chitam knew his journey was but the beginning of a greater saga — one that would shape the destiny of Calakmul and the legacy of its people. His resolve, now tempered with wisdom, would be his compass in the trials to come, guiding him in his role not just as a noble but as a beacon of hope in a world fraught with the shadows of war.

The cities of Calakmul and Tikal, once on the brink of war, found a new path forward, one of mutual respect and cooperation. And K'an Joy Chitam, once a noble hungry for victory, became a leader revered for his wisdom and courage, his legacy a testament to the power of understanding the true cost of war.

[CHAPTER 4] — AH MUZEN CAB

In the coastal city of Tulum, where the turquoise sea meets the dense green of the jungle, there lived a beekeeper named Ikal. His life was dedicated to the care of his hives, nestled within the vibrant flowers that adorned the cliffs overlooking the water. Ikal's bees were not just his livelihood; they were his connection to the divine, his way of honoring Ah Muzen Cab, the revered bee god who presided over bees and honey.

As the important ritual of the city approached, a ceremony that required vast amounts of honey to please the gods and ensure the community's prosperity, Ikal found himself in a precarious situation. One of his hives, the one he called Xunan after the ancient Mayan word for bee, was not producing enough honey. The rituals were sacred, and without the necessary honey, the blessings of the gods could not be secured.

Desperate, Ikal turned to prayer, offering incense and sweet fruits to Ah Muzen Cab, beseeching the deity's intervention to save Xunan and ensure the hive's productivity. Night after night, Ikal prayed, his heart heavy with the fear of disappointing his community and failing in his duty to the gods.

Then, one night, as the moon cast a silver glow over the sea, Ah Muzen Cab appeared before Ikal in a vision. The god, with his countenance reflecting the golden hues of honey, spoke to Ikal with a voice that buzzed like a thousand bees. "Ikal, devoted keeper of my sacred creatures, your prayers have been heard. But remember, the essence of life is balance and harmony. Speak to Xunan, share your worries and listen to the whispers of the bees. They will tell you what they need."

Ikal awoke from the vision with a heart full of hope. At dawn, he approached Xunan, speaking gently to the bees, sharing his fears and hopes. As he did, he noticed something he had overlooked before—the flowers around Xunan's hive were fewer, the jungle's encroachment limiting the bees' forage.

With newfound understanding, Ikal set to work, clearing the land around Xunan and planting more flowers, creating a haven for his bees. He spoke to them daily, his words a mix of prayer and promise, his actions guided by the wisdom Ah Muzen Cab had imparted.

As the days passed, Xunan thrived, the bees buzzing in harmony with Ikal's efforts. By the time of the ritual, Xunan's hive produced honey so abundant and sweet it seemed blessed by Ah Muzen Cab himself. The ceremony was a success, the community's joy and gratitude a balm to Ikal's soul.

In honoring Ah Muzen Cab's guidance, Ikal had not only saved Xunan but had also deepened his bond with his bees. He had learned the importance of listening, of harmony between the keeper and the kept, a lesson that extended beyond the hives to the world around him.

Tulum prospered, its rituals enriched by the honey from Ikal's hives. And Ikal, forever changed by his encounter with Ah Muzen Cab, continued his work with a heart full of reverence for the bees, the bearers of sweetness and life, under the watchful eyes of the bee god, whose presence in the hum of the hives whispered of the sacred dance between nature and the divine.

[CHAPTER 5] — AH PUCH

Dusk descended upon Chichen Itzá as the city's grand ball court, a marvel of stone that had witnessed countless cycles of the sun, prepared to host a game of Pok-Ta-Pok under the watchful eyes of both mortals and gods. The air was thick with anticipation, the crowd's breaths mingling with the scent of copal incense that veiled the arena in sacred smoke. Torches flared to life, casting flickering shadows over the I-shaped court, its sloped walls adorned with carvings that told of the game's divine heritage.

Two teams adorned in vibrant hues of jaguar skins and quetzal feathers took their places, their bodies marked with the symbols of their patron deities. The rubber ball, a sphere imbued with the essence of the cosmos itself, lay at the center, a silent testament to the gravity of the match to come. At a signal, a sound that echoed the heartbeat of the earth, the game commenced. The players moved with a grace and ferocity that belied the mortal coil, their hips striking the heavy ball in arcs that mimicked the journey of celestial bodies across the sky.

The clash of wills and the thud of rubber on stone filled the air, a symphony of human endeavor that reached its crescendo as the ball soared through the stone ring, a feat as rare as the alignment of planets. The crowd erupted in a roar, the victors' joy as palpable as the vanquished's despair. Yet, this triumph bore a weight heavier than the grandest of pyramids, for the victors' reward was a journey into the realm of Ah Puch, the god of death.

As the last rays of the sun bled away, swallowed by the voracious appetite of the night, the victors of the Pok-Ta-Pok game were led upwards, ascending the steep steps of the great pyramid that pierced the heavens above Chichen Itzá. Their steps, in unison, resonated against the stone, a march that echoed the pulsing heart of the earth itself. The crowd, a sea of shadowed faces, watched in reverent silence, their breaths held in anticipation of the sacred rite to come.

Atop the pyramid, under a canopy of stars that watched impassively, stood the priest, his figure a silhouette against the flickering torchlight. Adorned with the symbols of the gods and the weight of his office, he awaited the champions, the chosen ones whose victory had granted them a place of honor in the most hallowed of sacrifices.

The air was heavy with the scent of copal incense, its smoke curling upwards like the whispered prayers of the ancients. The victors approached the stone altar, their faces serene, touched by a solemnity that belied the fervor of their game. They had played for glory, for their city, for the favor of the gods, and now they stood ready to offer the ultimate tribute.

One by one, they lay upon the altar, their gazes fixed on the star-strewn sky, a tapestry of creation that stretched endlessly above. The priest, his voice a chant of ancient words, invoked the presence of the gods, calling upon Ah Puch, the lord of Xibalba, to accept these warriors into his realm.

With a hand that trembled not, the priest raised the obsidian knife, its edge catching the light of the torches, a shard of night itself. And as the blade descended, the victors met their end, not with fear but with a resolve that echoed the very essence of life itself. Their blood, a river of sacrifice, flowed down the pyramid's steps, a crimson tribute to the gods.

The crowd's silence broke, a murmur that grew into a chant, a vocal tribute to the bravery of the fallen and the cycle of life, death, and rebirth that governed all. The priest, his task completed, looked out over Chichen Itzá, his eyes seeing beyond the city, beyond the night, to the realm of Xibalba, where Ah Puch awaited the newest arrivals.

In the shadowy realm of Xibalba, Ah Puch awaited, his visage a tapestry of death's many facets. Around him swirled the rivers of blood and pus, and before him stretched the path of obstacles, each a test of strength, wisdom, and will. "Welcome, champions of the earthly realm," his voice echoed, a sound as chilling as the touch of night. "Your journey through my domain begins now. Only through facing the trials laid before you can you hope to find peace in the afterlife."

The trials were as harrowing as the myths foretold. The champions faced challenges that tested not just their physical prowess but the very fabric of their souls. They waded through rivers thick with the remnants of battles past, climbed mountains of jagged obsidian, and traversed forests where the trees whispered secrets meant to lead them astray.

Through it all, Ah Puch watched, his gaze impassive yet not without a glimmer of respect for the mortals who dared the darkness of his domain. For in their struggle, he saw the reflection of life itself — fraught with peril, yet beautiful in its resilience.

One by one, the champions met their end again, not in despair but in a realization that death was but a part of the cycle, a passage to a realm beyond fear and suffering. And as each soul found its peace, Ah Puch's realm grew richer, a testament to the courage and spirit of those who had played the game of life and death and emerged transcendent.

[CHAPTER 6] — AH TZUL

Clouds, heavy with the promise of rain, loomed over Copán, a city carved from the very heart of the earth, where the stones whispered ancient secrets, and the gods walked hidden paths. Amid this city of wonders, where pyramids reached for the heavens and the jungle encroached like an ever-watchful guardian, lived a boy named Hunacel. His was a life of simplicity, tending to the needs of his family's modest farm, yet his heart yearned for tales of the divine, for mysteries wrapped in the cloak of the jungle.

Hunacel's closest companion was a dog named Xan, whose loyalty knew no bounds, a creature of both the earth and, as Hunacel believed, a touch of the divine. Dogs were revered in Copán, seen as guides for souls wandering the treacherous paths to Xibalba, the underworld. It was said that Ah Tzul, the god of dogs, watched over these faithful creatures, his favor bestowed upon those who showed them kindness.

One evening, as the sun dipped below the horizon, painting the sky in hues of fire, Hunacel and Xan ventured beyond the farm's familiar borders, drawn by whispers of an ancient temple hidden deep within the jungle, a place where Ah Tzul was said to reside. The journey was perilous, the jungle alive with sounds of unseen creatures and the rustle of leaves that spoke of ancient enchantments.

As night embraced the world, Hunacel and Xan stumbled upon a clearing where ruins rose like specters, their stones entwined with the grip of the jungle. At the heart of these ruins stood a statue, not of stone, but of living vines, shaped into the form of a dog-headed deity: Ah Tzul himself.

The air thrummed with power as Ah Tzul's eyes, aglow with an otherworldly light, fixed upon Hunacel and Xan. "Why do you seek me, child of Copán?" the god's voice resonated, deep and commanding, yet not unkind.

Hunacel, his heart pounding with a mix of fear and awe, found the courage to speak. "Great Ah Tzul, protector of dogs, I seek your blessing for Xan, my loyal friend, and for all the dogs of Copán. They are more than companions; they are our guides, our protectors."

Ah Tzul's gaze softened as he regarded Xan, who sat by Hunacel's side, undaunted by the divine presence before him. "Your journey here speaks of bravery, and your request, of a pure heart. The dogs of Copán shall have my blessing, for they are the bridge between the mortal and the divine, the guides through darkness to the light beyond."

With a gesture from Ah Tzul, the vines began to move, weaving themselves into collars around Xan's neck, a symbol of the god's protection. "Let this collar be a sign of my favor, a protection for those who walk beside you."

As the first light of dawn broke through the canopy, Ah Tzul's form faded, leaving Hunacel and Xan alone in the clearing, the jungle around them suddenly serene, as if blessed by the god's presence. They returned to Copán as the sun rose, the city awakening to a new day.

In the days that followed, the dogs of Copán seemed to walk with a newfound grace, their eyes gleaming with a reflection of the divine. And though Hunacel never spoke of his encounter, those who looked upon Xan and saw the vine-woven collar knew that the boy and his dog had been touched by the gods. Xan, adorned with Ah Tzul's blessing, thrived alongside Hunacel, his life stretching beyond the span of ordinary canines. Together, they embarked on countless adventures, their bond a testament to the god's favor, a beacon of loyalty and friendship that illuminated their days.

As seasons turned and the stars shifted in their celestial dance, Hunacel grew from boy to man, his journey through life ever accompanied by Xan's steadfast presence. The people of Copán often whispered tales of the duo, their exploits becoming the stuff of legend, stories told under the canopy of night, beneath a sky scattered with the gods' watchful eyes.

Xan lived to an age that defied the natural order, his vitality unwavering, his spirit a constant source of joy for Hunacel. It was said that Ah Tzul himself had woven not just protection but the essence of life into the collar, granting Xan an extended tenure by his master's side.

When the time came for Hunacel to tread the path all mortals must walk, a path that led beyond the veil of this world, he did so with a heart full of gratitude for the years granted to him. Xan, ever loyal, lay beside Hunacel, his eyes holding the light of countless sunrises and sunsets they had witnessed together.

As Hunacel drew his final breath, it was in the comfort of knowing that his life had been a journey shared with a friend bestowed upon him by the gods. Xan, his loyal companion, passed peacefully with him, their spirits entwined in departure as they had been in life, guided by Ah Tzul's silent vigil to the realms beyond.

[CHAPTER 7] — AHAU CHAMAHEZ

Beneath the canopy of a sky jeweled with stars, the city of Quirigua lay enshrouded in a silence broken only by the whispered prayers of those seeking solace and healing. Among them was a healer named Ixchel, named after the goddess of the moon, though her gifts stemmed from another divine source—Ahau Chamahez, the god of medicine and healing. Ixchel's reputation as a healer had grown far and wide, her remedies and knowledge seemingly boundless, drawing the sick and wounded not just from Quirigua but from distant cities across the Mayan lands.

Yet, Ixchel harbored a secret. Her power was not entirely her own. It was on a night much like this, many years ago, that Ahau Chamahez had appeared before her, as if conjured from the very air itself, his presence commanding yet imbued with a tranquility that stilled her very soul. His visage, noble and serene, bore the marks of eternity, eyes that had witnessed the cycles of the moon countless times over.

"Daughter of Quirigua," he had begun, his voice a melody that seemed to harmonize with the very heartbeat of the earth, "your path is chosen, and your hands blessed. The gifts I bestow upon you are ancient, as old as the roots that cradle the heart of the earth."

Ixchel, awestruck, had found the courage to speak, her voice a whisper in the presence of divinity. "Great Ahau Chamahez, how am I to wield such gifts? The weight of such power is immense."

Ahau Chamahez had smiled, a gesture that seemed to light up the darkness. "With wisdom, Ixchel. With compassion and reverence for the balance of life. You are not the master of these gifts but their steward. Listen to the plants, for they are your allies. Respect the ailments, for they are teachers. And above all, cherish the lives of those you heal, for they are the greatest gift."

With those words, Ahau Chamahez had faded into the night, leaving Ixchel transformed. Her hands, once uncertain, now moved with purpose and grace, each remedy a testament to the god's teachings. She had become a conduit for his healing light, a guardian of the balance he spoke of. From that day forth, Ixchel found her hands guided by a force beyond her understanding, her concoctions imbued with a potency that spoke of divine intervention.

On this particular night, a young boy named K'in had been brought to her doorstep, his body wracked with fever, his spirit teetering on the edge of the underworld. His parents, eyes brimming with tears, pleaded for

Ixchel's intervention. As she prepared her space with incense and the symbols of Ahau Chamahez, Ixchel felt a familiar presence envelop the room, a warmth that promised hope amidst despair.

Tonight, as Ixchel prepared her potions, she felt his presence once more, not as a vision, but as a comforting assurance that she was not alone. The fire before her flickered, casting a glow that seemed to echo the divine light she had once beheld.

"Ahau Chamahez," she spoke softly into the night, "I am forever your servant, guided by your wisdom. May my hands bring healing, may my heart bring hope."

Drawing upon the knowledge bestowed upon her by the god of healing, Ixchel worked tirelessly through the night, her hands deftly mixing herbs and chanting incantations that seemed to resonate with the very fabric of the universe. As dawn painted the sky with hues of gold and crimson, a miracle unfolded. K'in's fever broke, his breaths deepened, and color returned to his cheeks. The boy, once lost to the shadows, was returned to the world of the living.

The people of Quirigua whispered among themselves, their words a mixture of awe and reverence. They spoke not just of Ixchel's gift but of the divine presence that seemed to linger around her, a testament to the favor of Ahau Chamahez. Ixchel, however, knew that her gift was not for personal glory but for the service of others. She was but a vessel through which the god of healing worked his will.

Years passed, and Ixchel's life unfolded like the petals of a flower under the sun. She trained others in the art of healing, sharing the knowledge that Ahau Chamahez had imparted upon her. And when her time came, as all things must, she passed into the next world with a heart full of peace, her legacy a tapestry of lives mended and spirits restored.

In the heart of Quirigua, a statue stood in her honor, a figure of a woman with hands outstretched, offering healing to all who sought it. And though the statue was of stone, those who gazed upon it could swear they felt the warmth of a divine presence, a reminder of the bond between the god Ahau Chamahez and the people he protected through the hands of a humble healer.

[CHAPTER 8] — AHAU KIN

Shadows lengthened across the limestone facades of Yaxchilán, where the Usumacinta River whispered secrets of ages past. In this city, where the sun's journey was observed with reverence, lived a young scribe named Itzamna, whose heart was as vast as the sky. Itzamna's days were spent etching the history of his people into stone, but his nights belonged to the study of stars and the endless cycle of day into night.

Itzamna was particularly drawn to the mysteries of Ahau Kin, the sun god who painted the sky with hues of gold and crimson as he journeyed to the underworld each evening. The young scribe longed to understand the divine essence of the setting sun, its beauty a fleeting whisper between the realms of light and shadow.

One evening, as the sun dipped low, bleeding colors that no stone could hold, Itzamna ventured to the edge of the river, where the boundary between the worlds felt thin. There, he called out to Ahau Kin, his voice a blend of hope and desperation, seeking the wisdom of the ages.

As the last sliver of sun kissed the horizon goodbye, the air around Itzamna shimmered, and Ahau Kin appeared before him, not as a fearsome deity, but as a figure cloaked in the warm glow of dusk. His presence was both a comfort and an awe-inspiring force, his eyes reflecting the infinite cycle of endings and beginnings.

"Ahau Kin," Itzamna began, his voice steady despite the pounding of his heart, "why does your journey to the underworld bring such beauty to the sky? Why does the setting sun stir such longing in the hearts of those who watch?"

Ahau Kin smiled, his voice the sound of sunlight moving across the earth. "Itzamna, devoted scribe, the beauty of the setting sun is a reminder of the cycles of life, of the balance between light and darkness. It is a moment of reflection, a bridge between what has been and what will be."

The god then reached out, touching Itzamna's forehead. Visions flooded the young scribe's mind: the sun's arduous journey through the underworld, the challenges it faced, and its triumphant rise each morning, reborn. Itzamna saw the world through the eyes of the sun god, every sunset a farewell, every sunrise a promise.

"Your longing," Ahau Kin continued, "is the soul's recognition of its own eternal journey, mirroring mine across the sky. Embrace the beauty of endings, for they precede new beginnings. Your work, your words, are part of this cycle, etching the stories of today for the suns of tomorrow."

As the vision faded and Ahau Kin's figure dissolved into the twilight, Itzamna was left on the banks of the Usumacinta, the night now a cloak of velvet around him. The young scribe returned to Yaxchilán, his heart alight with new understanding.

Itzamna's work took on a new depth, his etchings capturing not just the events of his time, but the cyclical nature of existence itself, inspired by the god of the setting sun. And though he never again saw Ahau Kin in form, he felt the god's presence each evening as the sky bloomed with color, a daily reminder of the divine cycle of endings and beginnings, of the beauty and wisdom found in the setting sun.

[CHAPTER 9] — AJBIT

In the dawn of the world, when the earth was still a canvas of possibility, Ajbit, one of the revered creator gods, embarked on a divine quest to fill the void with beings capable of praise, thought, and love. His workshop was the cosmos, his materials the essence of the earth itself.

The first attempt was with mud. Ajbit, with hands shaped by eternity, molded figures with care, envisioning beings that would dance under the sun and sing praises to the creators. But these mud creatures were fragile, dissolving back into the earth with the first rain. "Water gives life, yet it undoes my work," Ajbit mused, watching his creations crumble. "Perhaps the very essence of life is not in its permanence, but in its ability to leave a mark, however fleeting."

Undeterred, Ajbit delved deeper into the fabric of creation, seeking a material that balanced delicacy with resilience. His gaze fell upon obsidian, the volcanic glass that mirrored the night sky's depth. From obsidian, he sculpted figures sleek and strong, their bodies gleaming like stars against the velvet dark. But these beings were too rigid, their hearts as impenetrable as the stone from which they were hewn. They stood silent and unyielding, unable to embrace or be embraced.

Next, Ajbit turned to wood, carving figures with intricate detail, infusing them with the breath of life. These wooden beings walked and worked, but their eyes were void of understanding, their hearts empty of gratitude. "They move, yet they do not feel," Ajbit pondered, his heart heavy with disappointment. "To create beings in the truest sense, they must possess more than mere motion; they must have spirit, a connection to the divine."

In his quest for the perfect creation, Ajbit experimented with other materials, each attempt a reflection of his growing understanding. He tried creating beings from leaves, hoping their rustling whispers would evolve into language and song. Yet, they were too ephemeral, scattering with the wind, leaving no more than a whisper behind. "Beauty and grace they possess, yet they lack the strength to endure," Ajbit reflected, his resolve unwavering. "The essence of life must balance delicacy with resilience."

Then, there was an attempt with clay, figures that held promise with their solid form and enduring presence. But they cracked under the sun's relentless gaze, their silence a stark reminder of what was still missing. "Strength alone is not enough," Ajbit realized. "There must be flexibility, an ability to adapt and grow. True life is dynamic, ever-changing."

With each attempt, Ajbit's understanding deepened, his vision clearer. It was in the golden fields of maize that inspiration struck, the staple of life for all who would come to inhabit the earth. Maize, with its cycles of death and rebirth, held the secrets of life itself. Ajbit crafted beings from maize dough, shaping them with the lessons learned from his previous attempts. These beings stood tall, their eyes alight with the spark of consciousness, their hearts capable of love and reverence.

As Ajbit breathed life into these maize creations, he saw in their eyes the reflection of the cosmos, a connection to the divine that had eluded his earlier works. "In maize, I have found the balance," Ajbit mused, a sense of fulfillment filling his being. "Not only does it sustain the body, but it also nourishes the soul. These beings are my true children, capable of understanding the cycles of life, of sustaining the balance of the cosmos."

The creation of humanity from maize was Ajbit's triumph, a culmination of divine effort and understanding. These beings flourished, their voices filling the world with songs of praise and gratitude, their hands working the earth, their spirits connected to the divine.

And though Ajbit continued to watch over humanity, guiding and teaching, he often reflected on the journey of creation. Each failed attempt was a step toward understanding, a testament to the complexity of life. In the end, it was the combination of resilience and spirit, matter and divine spark, that embodied the essence of true life. Through the maize beings, Ajbit's vision was realized, a creation that could honor the gods, cherish the earth, and understand the sacred cycle of life and death.

[CHAPTER 10] — AWILIX

Deep within the heart of the verdant jungle that blankets the highlands, where the mists weave tales of mystery and the unseen, there thrived a realm under the watchful gaze of the K'iche' gods. Among them, Awilix, the male deity of the moon, revered as a protector in the guise of a mighty jaguar, held a special place in the hearts of the K'iche' nobility. His domain was the night, a realm of shadow and silver light, where he roamed as both guardian and guide.

In this age of splendor and strife, there lived a noble of the K'iche' lineage named Tecun. Brave and wise beyond his years, Tecun was destined for greatness, his path intertwined with the will of the gods. Yet, destiny is a road paved with trials, and Tecun's journey was to be no exception. Word had spread among the neighboring tribes of his rising power, and with envy, dark plans were woven to halt his ascent.

One night, under a moon veiled by the whispers of conspiring clouds, Tecun ventured alone into the jungle. A message, cryptic and urgent, had called him forth, promising knowledge that would secure his people's future. The jungle, alive with the chorus of the night, seemed to watch in silent anticipation as Tecun moved deeper into its heart.

Unbeknownst to Tecun, the message was a ruse, a trap laid by his enemies to ensnare him in a place where even his courageous heart and keen blade might not prevail. As he navigated the dense underbrush, a sudden rustle froze him in his tracks. From the shadows emerged a jaguar, its coat a tapestry of the night itself, eyes glowing with an ethereal light. Tecun, poised for battle, sensed something divine in the creature's gaze, a wisdom and power that far surpassed the natural world.

"I am Awilix," the jaguar spoke, its voice a deep rumble that resonated with the very soul of the jungle. "You walk a perilous path, Tecun, son of the K'iche'. Enemies seek your downfall, but I have watched over you since your birth under the moon's benevolent light. Tonight, I shall guard you as my own."

With Awilix by his side, Tecun felt a courage that surged like the rivers during the rain. The jaguar, a manifestation of Awilix's divine will, led Tecun through the jungle, their steps silent as the night breeze. They encountered the ambush, a band of warriors shrouded in malice and shadow, but with Awilix's might, they were no match. The deity, in his jaguar form, was a specter of moonlit retribution, swift and lethal.

As dawn's first light pierced the veil of darkness, the jungle stood in quiet testament to the night's events. Tecun, standing amidst the clearing, looked upon Awilix with reverence and gratitude. "How may I honor you, great Awilix, who has protected me with the ferocity and grace of the moon's own light?"

"Live with the strength and wisdom you have shown this night," Awilix replied, the first rays of dawn reflecting in his luminous eyes. "Protect your people, as I have protected you. Let your rule be guided by the balance between light and shadow, strength and compassion. This is the honor I seek."

With those words, Awilix vanished into the jungle, leaving Tecun alone but for the story that would echo through the ages. The noble returned to his people, his rule marked by the virtues Awilix had bestowed upon him, and his legend grew, a tale of divine guardianship and a noble's unyielding spirit.

[CHAPTER 11] — BACABS

Deep within the heart of the verdant Yucatan, where the dense canopy whispered ancient secrets and the air thrummed with the life force of the jungle, there existed a village that thrived under the benevolent watch of the Bacabs. In this village lived a farmer named Tzakol, his life was bound to the soil and the cycles of the heavens.

Tzakol's crops were the envy of the region, flourishing with a vitality that seemed almost divine. This prosperity was no mere chance, for Tzakol held a deep reverence for the Bacabs, honoring them through rituals and offerings, understanding their vital role in the balance of nature. He knew well that the Bacabs, each guarding a corner of the world, were the keepers of the seasons and the stewards of the earth's fertility.

As the dry season stretched longer than memory could recall, threatening the survival of the village, Tzakol set out into the jungle, seeking the favor of the Bacabs to bring the much-needed rain. His journey led him to the ruins of an ancient temple, hidden from the eyes of the uninitiated, a place where the veil between the mortal world and that of the gods was at its thinnest.

Here, under the open sky, Tzakol called to the Bacabs, his voice a blend of desperation and hope. As the night deepened, a remarkable event unfolded — the Bacabs answered. Emerging from the cardinal points they guarded, their forms were majestic, each embodying the essence of their domain. To the north appeared the Bacab of the white winds, his presence stirring a cool breeze that whispered of coming change. From the south, the Bacab of yellow fire brought warmth, a promise of the sun's return. The east saw the arrival of the red Bacab, herald of the sunrise and the renewal of life. Lastly, from the west, the black Bacab emerged, his essence carrying the nourishment of rain-filled clouds.

"Tzakol, devoted one," they spoke in unison, their voices a harmony that resonated with the very heartbeat of the earth, "your reverence has been noted, and your plea heard. The balance shall be restored."

With a collective gesture, the Bacabs summoned the elements they commanded. From the east, the sun's rays pierced the morning fog, from the south, the warmth spread across the land, from the north, a refreshing wind began to blow, and from the west, dark clouds gathered, heavy with the promise of rain.

Tzakol watched in awe as the first drops of rain fell upon his upturned face, a blessing from the heavens that soon became a downpour, drenching the parched earth, ensuring that the crops would not only survive but thrive. The Bacabs, their task complete, faded back into the elements from which they came, leaving behind a world renewed.

The village celebrated this miracle, their joy a testament to the power and benevolence of the Bacabs. Tzakol, however, knew that their favor was not to be taken for granted. He vowed to continue his rituals and offerings, to live in harmony with the natural world, and to teach his children the importance of reverence for the Bacabs, the guardians of the world's corners.

[CHAPTER 12] — BITOL

Amidst the cosmic void, where silence reigned supreme and the fabric of existence lay untouched, the first stirrings of creation whispered across the abyss. Bitol, the architect of worlds, moved within this nothingness, his presence a beacon of intent in the vast emptiness. Not bound by form nor confined to the realms of the known, Bitol's essence was the spark that sought to illuminate the darkness, to bring forth order from the chaos.

With a thought, Bitol envisioned a sphere, suspended in the void, a canvas upon which the story of life could unfold. This sphere began to pulse with potential, its surface a barren expanse yearning for the touch of the divine. Bitol, whose wisdom spanned the ages, saw not just the physical form of this nascent world but the intricate web of life that it was destined to support.

He reached into the heart of the void, gathering the elements that would sow the seeds of creation. With water, he carved rivers and oceans, their depths a mirror to the skies. With earth, he raised mountains and valleys, sculpting the land with a gentle yet firm hand. Air swirled at his command, breathing movement into the stillness, and fire brought warmth, a promise of the sun's embrace.

Yet Bitol's vision extended beyond the mere shaping of land and sea. He imbued this world with the essence of time, setting the stars in motion and defining the cycles of day and night, of seasons that whispered of change and growth. Each action, each creation, was a note in a symphony of complexity and beauty, a testament to Bitol's mastery and care.

Bitol's creation was not yet complete. The god knew that true beauty lay in diversity, in the myriad forms of life that would inhabit this world. Thus, Bitol spoke again, and the earth stirred. From the fertile soil sprang forth the first blades of grass, the first blossoming flowers, each a testament to the world's inherent magic. Trees reached for the heavens, their branches a shelter for the creatures yet to come.

The waters teemed with life, from the smallest plankton to the great leviathans that danced through the deep. The skies, too, found their voice, as birds took to the air, their songs a melody that spoke of freedom and the joy of existence.

Bitol watched as the world blossomed, a living masterpiece that pulsed with the rhythm of life itself. Yet, the creator god knew that creation was an act of sharing, that this world, in all its beauty, was not meant to exist in solitude.

Thus, Bitol summoned the other gods, each a master of their domain, to witness the birth of this world. Together, they stood at the edge of creation, their presence a testament to the unity and diversity of the divine.

"Behold," Bitol proclaimed, voice resonating with the force of creation, "a world of boundless beauty and endless potential. Let this be a place of harmony, where life flourishes in all its forms."

The gods marveled at Bitol's creation, each finding a reflection of their essence within the world's intricate design. They knew that this world, vibrant and alive, was a gift of unparalleled value, a treasure to be guarded and cherished.

Bitol then retreated into the silence from which he had emerged, his presence woven into the very essence of the world, leaving the other gods to do with it as they would.

[CHAPTER 13] — BOLON TZACAB

Amid the grandeur of Piedras Negras, where the Usumacinta River carves its way through the land, a crisis of succession threatened to unravel the fabric of the kingdom. The air was thick with tension, as whispers of doubt and claims of illegitimacy clung to the newly ascended ruler, Xbalanque, a young noble whose lineage, though noble, was clouded by the sudden and mysterious demise of his predecessor.

In this time of uncertainty, Xbalanque sought to solidify his claim to the throne, to quell the murmurs of dissent among his people and the nobility. His thoughts turned to Bolon Tzacab, the god whose domain was the very essence of divine kingship and whose favor was essential for the legitimacy of rulers. Xbalanque knew well that to secure his reign, he must seek the god's blessing, a sign that would be recognized by all as divine sanction.

Meanwhile, in the shadows of the great pyramids, a stone carver named Ixkun labored, his hands skilled in the art of shaping the limestone into stelae that told the stories of kings and gods. His work was a bridge between the mortal and the divine, a record of the celestial favor bestowed upon the rulers of Piedras Negras.

The moment came when Xbalanque summoned Ixkun to his presence, commissioning a stela that would not only depict his ascension but also invoke the endorsement of Bolon Tzacab himself. Ixkun, understanding the weight of this task, set out to create a masterpiece that would echo through the ages.

As Ixkun chiseled away, shaping the narrative in stone, a vision came to him. Bolon Tzacab appeared, his form as regal as the kings he legitimized, wielding the symbols of power and fertility that underscored his authority. The god spoke, his voice resonating with the force of thunder, "Ixkun, through your hands, my will is made manifest. Let this stela be a testament to my favor upon Xbalanque. His right to rule is ordained by the cosmos."

Emboldened by the vision, Ixkun worked with renewed fervor, his tools guided by divine inspiration. The stela he created was unlike any other, a marvel that captured Bolon Tzacab's majestic form alongside Xbalanque, a celestial endorsement carved in stone.

Upon its unveiling in the central plaza of Piedras Negras, the stela silenced all doubts regarding Xbalanque's legitimacy. The people and nobility alike marveled at the depiction, the divine sanction clear for all to see. Bolon Tzacab's presence loomed large, a reminder of the god's role in the order of the cosmos and the earthly realm.

Xbalanque's reign was thus secured, his rule marked by prosperity and peace, under the watchful gaze of Bolon Tzacab. And Ixkun, the stone carver, was honored as a conduit of the divine will, his work a bridge between the heavens and the earth.

[CHAPTER 14] — CAMAZOTZ

Shadows stretched across Kaminaljuyú as twilight whispered the day into slumber, the ancient city a silhouette against the fading light. Among its maze of stone and thatch, a sculptor named Yalitza lay restless, her dreams a canvas for the fears that daylight kept at bay. That night, her spirit wandered far, drawn into the depths of Zotzilaha, the realm of Camazotz, where darkness reigned eternal and the echo of wings was a harbinger of death.

In this nightmare, Yalitza found herself in a vast cavern, the air thick with the musk of decay. The sound of her heartbeat, a drum of terror in the oppressive silence, seemed to summon the denizens of this dark world. From the shadows, Camazotz emerged, a deity of night and death, his form a grotesque fusion of man and bat, eyes gleaming with an unholy light. His wings unfolded like the very gates of Xibalba, casting a chill that seeped into the marrow.

"Who dares to tread the sacred halls of Zotzilaha?" Camazotz's voice thundered, a sound that vibrated through the cavernous expanse.

Frozen with fear, Yalitza mustered her courage, her voice a mere whisper against the darkness. "I am but a dreamer, lost in the weave of night. I seek no trespass in your domain."

Camazotz circled her, a predator gauging its prey, his presence a suffocating weight. "All who wander here face the trials of the night. Your craft bears the mark of creation, but here, you shall know destruction. Will you cower in the shadows, or will your resolve shine brighter than the fear that binds you?"

The challenge hung heavy in the air, and Yalitza, understanding the peril of her situation, called upon the deepest wells of her spirit. She envisioned her sculptures, creations born of stone and imbued with the essence of life, their forms defiant against the entropy that Camazotz embodied.

With a clarity that pierced the veil of her fear, Yalitza spoke, "In the world above, my creations stand against the passage of time, a testament to the light that endures in the face of darkness. Here, in your realm, I stand with the same resolve. My art is my shield, my creativity my spear."

Camazotz, intrigued by the sculptor's defiance, offered a challenge. "Bring forth your art in the heart of darkness, and you shall find your path to dawn."

The nightmare shifted, the darkness coalescing into stone before Yalitza. With hands guided by an unseen force, she sculpted as she never had before, her creation a beacon in the oppressive gloom. As she worked, the cavern around her began to illuminate, shadows retreating from the light of her artistry.

When her task was complete, Yalitza beheld her creation — a sculpture of Camazotz himself, not as a figure of fear, but as a guardian of the balance between life and death, his wings outstretched not in menace but in protection of the cycles that governed all existence.

Camazotz, observing the transformation of his visage through Yalitza's eyes, acknowledged her victory. "Your art has brought light to the darkness, sculptor. Your path to dawn is earned."

Yalitza awoke in Kaminaljuyú, the first light of dawn caressing her face. The nightmare had passed, but the lesson remained. In her hands and heart, she carried the power to confront darkness, to transform fear into creation. Her sculptures, henceforth, carried a deeper essence, a reminder of her journey through the night and the resilience required to face the perils within and beyond.

And in the realm of Zotzilaha, the sculpture still stands as a testament to the night a mortal dared to challenge the darkness, a symbol of the enduring light of the human spirit.

[CHAPTER 15] — CHAAC

Dawn broke over Aguateca, casting a golden hue over the sprawling maize fields that fed the city. In this place, where the earth kissed the sky, lived a farmer named Hunac, whose reverence for Chaac shaped the rhythm of his life. Hunac knew well that the prosperity of his crops was a gift from the gods, particularly Chaac, whose lightning nourished the earth and brought the rains that quenched the thirst of every stalk of maize.

Each morning, as the first light of dawn crept across the land, Hunac stood at the edge of his fields, offering prayers and incense to Chaac. He understood the god's dual nature: a giver of life and a wielder of destructive power, symbolized by the serpentine axe that could either bestow fertility or wreak havoc.

One season, as the dry spell stretched longer than any before, the fields of Aguateca began to wither, the maize stalks bowing their heads in surrender to the scorching sun. The people grew anxious, their hearts heavy with the fear of famine. Hunac, however, held onto his faith, planning a grand gesture to appeal to Chaac's favor.

Gathering his strength, Hunac embarked on a journey to the heart of the jungle, seeking a sacred cenote known to be a conduit to the gods. There, surrounded by the whispers of ancient trees, Hunac offered his most precious possession: a jade figurine of Chaac, hoping to catch the deity's attention.

As the figurine disappeared into the dark waters of the cenote, the air around Hunac charged, a palpable tension that preluded the divine. Chaac manifested before him, not in wrath, but in a form that radiated the formidable power of the heavens. His serpentine leg rooted him to the earth, while his eyes, like storm clouds, bore into Hunac's soul.

"Hunac, why do you summon me with such fervor?" the deity's voice boomed, echoing against the stone walls of the cenote.

Hunac, though trembling, found his voice. "Great Chaac, Aguateca withers under the sun. I beg of you, bring us rain. Let your lightning touch the earth and give life to our crops."

Chaac regarded the farmer, his expression a tempest of thought. "Your faith is strong, Hunac. You understand the balance of life and destruction I wield. For this, Aguateca shall not suffer."

With a raise of his axe, the sky darkened, lightning shot out of it towards the sky and the first rumblings of thunder rolled across the heavens. Chaac disappeared as swiftly as he had come, leaving Hunac alone as the first drops of rain began to fall, gentle at first, then growing into a deluge that sang of life renewed.

Hunac returned to Aguateca, his heart light with the promise of Chaac's gift. In the weeks that followed, the maize fields of Aguateca stood tall and green, a testament to the god's power and the farmer's unwavering faith.

The people of Aguateca celebrated their bountiful harvest with offerings of gratitude to Chaac, their prayers mixing with the scent of fresh maize. Hunac, however, offered something more: a vow to honor Chaac not just in times of need, but in every moment of abundance, understanding that the god's blessings were as much a part of the cycle of life as the seasons themselves.

[CHAPTER 16] — CHIN

In the heart of the dense jungle that envelops Dos Pilas, where the whispers of the ancients still echo through the towering ceiba trees, lived two men, Ahuil and K'inich. Their bond, profound and unwavering, was a testament to the love that dared to flourish in the shadows of societal norms. Yet, in a world governed by the rigid expectations of roles and relationships, their union was viewed with skepticism and disdain.

Ahuil, a skilled weaver whose tapestries captured the vibrant hues of the Mayan world, and K'inich, a warrior whose prowess in battle was sung by poets, found in each other a sanctuary, a place where the spirit soared free and the heart knew no bounds. But this sanctuary was a fragile haven, threatened by the whispers of disapproval that rustled like dry leaves in the wind.

The tension reached its zenith during the K'atun celebration, a time when the community gathered to honor the gods and the cycles of time. Amidst the festivities, the love between Ahuil and K'inich became the subject of scorn, casting a shadow over the joyous occasion. It was then, under the cloak of night, when the moon cast a silvery glow over the stone pyramids of Dos Pilas, that Chin appeared before them.

Chin, the deity associated with homosexual relationships, emerged not with the fury of a tempest but with the serene grace of the evening star. His presence was a balm to Ahuil and K'inich's troubled hearts, his visage bearing neither judgment nor reproof but an understanding that spanned the ages.

"Why do you weep in the moon's embrace, when your love is a gift bestowed by the heavens?" Chin's voice, gentle as the breeze that stirs the maize fields, enveloped them.

Ahuil, his voice trembling with emotion, spoke of the scorn they faced, of the love that dared not speak its name under the watchful eyes of society. K'inich stood by his side, a silent sentinel, his resolve fortified by Chin's presence.

Chin listened, his eyes reflecting the tapestry of human emotions, then spoke, "In the vast expanse of the cosmos, where stars are born and fade, love is the constant light that guides us through the darkness. Your bond is a reflection of the divine, a river that flows unabated, nourished by the very essence of life."

With a wave of his hand, Chin bestowed upon them a blessing, a radiant light that enveloped Ahuil and K'inich, sealing their union with the sanctity of the divine. And to the people of Dos Pilas, Chin proclaimed,

"Let their love be a beacon, a testament to the myriad forms of affection that enrich our world. For in love, we find the reflection of the gods."

As Chin vanished, leaving behind a world touched by the divine, the people of Dos Pilas saw Ahuil and K'inich through new eyes. The warriors who once scorned K'inich now stood by him, their weapons raised in salute. The weavers who whispered against Ahuil now sought his guidance, their hands eager to learn from his mastery.

Ahuil and K'inich's love, once a source of division, became a bridge, uniting the community in a newfound understanding of love's boundless nature. And in the tapestries that Ahuil wove, in the battles that K'inich fought, the blessing of Chin was ever present, a reminder that love, in all its forms, is a divine gift, worthy of reverence and celebration.

In Dos Pilas, under the watchful eyes of the gods, Ahuil and K'inich lived their days, their love a legend that would echo through the ages, a story of courage, acceptance, and the divine affirmation of love's power to transcend.

[CHAPTER 17] — CHITAM

In the shadowed confines of Altun Ha, where the grandeur of ancient stones bore silent witness to both the zenith of Mayan civilization and the depths of human despair, lived Nayeli. Her spirit, a beacon of resilience in the enveloping darkness, flickered under the harsh reality of her existence. Captured during a raid on her village, Nayeli found herself in the clutches of a destiny she had never imagined, condemned to serve as a sex slave, her dignity stolen away night after night.

It was in these moments of deepest sorrow that Nayeli's prayers pierced the veil between the mortal realm and the divine, reaching the ears of Chitam, the god of prisoners. Unlike the warriors who sought glory in the heat of battle or the rulers who yearned for the gods' favor to legitimize their reign, Nayeli asked for neither victory nor validation but for deliverance from the darkness that had claimed her.

Chitam, moved by the purity and fervor of her plea, manifested before her, a presence as formidable as it was compassionate. "Why do you call to me, Nayeli, child of misfortune?" His voice, a soothing balm to her frayed soul, offered a glimmer of hope amidst the despair.

With a courage born of desperation, Nayeli shared the tale of her anguish, of a life fractured by the whims of those who saw her not as a person but as a possession. "I seek a path to freedom," she implored, "a chance to reclaim the fragments of my spirit scattered in the darkness."

Chitam, god of those bound by chains unseen, bestowed upon Nayeli a gift unlike any other—the strength to endure, to rise above the torment of her existence, and to weave the shards of her shattered spirit into a tapestry of resilience. "Your journey, Nayeli, is far from over. Within you lies the power to redefine your destiny, to transform your pain into a wellspring of strength. Freedom is not merely the absence of chains. It is the strength to redefine your fate, the courage to face tomorrow with hope."

Empowered by Chitam's divine intervention, Nayeli's resolve hardened like obsidian. In the days that followed, her spirit, once dimmed by the cruelty of her captors, began to shine with an inner light that could not be extinguished. It was then that a warrior named Tecun, whose life had been shaped by the rigid codes of warfare and honor, saw in Nayeli not a captive to be scorned, but a spirit as fierce as the jaguar that roamed the jungles surrounding Altun Ha. It was a recognition that defied the norms of their world, a spark that threatened to ignite a fire in the hearts of both captive and captor.

Witnessing the transformation wrought by her indomitable will, he was moved by a respect that blossomed into an unlikely love — a love that dared to flourish in the unlikeliest of soils. Tecun sought her forgiveness for the injustices she had endured. In the sanctity of their burgeoning bond, he offered her not chains but a promise — a promise of protection, of companionship, and of a shared future.

Chitam whispered courage into Tecun's heart, urging him to defy convention, to embrace a destiny of his own making. Moved by a force he could neither deny nor explain, Tecun declared his intention to take Nayeli as his wife, to offer her not the chains of captivity but the bonds of love. It was a decision that challenged the expectations of their people, a daring leap into the unknown that required the blessing of the gods.

Before the elders and the spirits of their ancestors, Tecun and Nayeli stood hand in hand, their gaze defiant yet hopeful. In that moment, Chitam manifested, his presence a silent testament to the power of the human heart to overcome the shadows of fate. With Chitam's silent blessing, Nayeli and Tecun forged a new path together, one built on the foundations of mutual respect and understanding. Their union, a testament to the transformative power of love and resilience, became a beacon of hope for those who had known only despair.

In time, Nayeli and Tecun's story was etched into the very stones of Altun Ha, a legacy immortalized not in tales of conquest or dominion, but in the enduring whispers of redemption and the unbreakable bonds of the human spirit. And though the age of gods and mortals ebbed and flowed like the tides of time, the tale of Nayeli's journey from slave into the embrace of love remained, a timeless ode to the strength found in the depths of the human heart.

[CHAPTER 18] — CIZIN

Amid the towering pyramids of Tikal, where the jungle's embrace concealed the whispers of the ancients, the life of a warrior named Balam came to its twilight. His days, once filled with the glory of battle and the warmth of the sun, now ebbed away within the confines of his stone dwelling, the rhythms of a life lived fully giving way to the silence of approaching death.

Balam, whose name meant 'jaguar,' had been a protector of Tikal, a fierce warrior whose prowess on the battlefield was matched only by his devotion to the gods. Yet, as the shadows lengthened and the light of his life dimmed, it was not the gods of sun or rain to whom his thoughts turned, but to Cizin, the lord of the underworld, the one who would guide his passage into the realm beyond.

As the end drew near, the air in Balam's chamber grew thick, a palpable tension that preluded the arrival of the deity. And then, with the suddenness of a storm breaking upon the canopy, Cizin appeared. His form was as the stories had foretold: a skeletal figure, draped in the vestiges of decay, his necklace of human eyes a grim testament to his dominion over death. The stench of the underworld accompanied him, filling the room with the odors of a world unseen but deeply feared.

"Balam, mighty warrior of Tikal," Cizin's voice echoed, a sound like the rustling of dry leaves. "Your time among the living draws to a close. I have come to guide you to the realm that awaits beyond the veil of mortality."

Balam, his strength waning, faced Cizin with the dignity of a warrior meeting his final adversary. "I have lived with honor, fought with valor. I fear not the journey that lies ahead."

Cizin, the Stinking One, regarded Balam with an inscrutable gaze, then spoke, "Your bravery has marked your days, warrior. But the path through Xibalba is fraught with trials, a reflection of the life you have led, the deeds you have done."

Balam, his resolve unshaken, replied, "I stand ready to face what comes, to walk the path laid out before me."

With a nod that seemed to acknowledge Balam's courage, Cizin extended a bony hand, the air shimmering around him. "Then come, Balam. Let us walk together into the darkness, where your spirit will be tested and your heart weighed."

And so, Balam, the great warrior of Tikal, took his final breath, his spirit stepping forth into the unknown. As Cizin led him away, the room grew still once more, the passage of the warrior marked by the lingering scent of the underworld.

In Tikal, the tale of Balam's departure became a story told in hushed tones, a reminder of the inevitable journey that awaits all mortals. And though Cizin was feared as the lord of death, in the tale of Balam's passing, there was a recognition of the respect accorded to a life well-lived, the acknowledgment that even in death, the strength of the human spirit endures.

[CHAPTER 19] — CIT BOLOM TUM

As dawn painted the sky with the first light, the vast city of Kan, known to the future as El Mirador, awakened to the sounds of the bustling market and the distant calls of the howler monkeys from the dense jungle that surrounded it. Among its inhabitants was a young healer named Kinich, whose knowledge of herbs and healing practices was surpassed only by his devotion to Cit Bolon Tum, the revered god of medicine and healing.

Kinich's reputation as a healer had spread far and wide, drawing the sick and injured from all corners of the city to his modest dwelling near the Great Plaza. Despite his skills, there was one ailment that eluded Kinich's grasp, a mysterious fever that had claimed many lives and now threatened the life of the city's esteemed ruler, Ahau Ixik.

As Ahau Ixik lay delirious, the city's priests and healers gathered in solemn assembly, their prayers ascending to the heavens for divine intervention. Kinich, however, sought a more direct appeal. Under the cloak of night, he ventured into the heart of the jungle, to a sacred cenote known only to the most devout followers of Cit Bolon Tum.

Standing at the water's edge, Kinich called upon the god with an offering of copal incense and jade, his voice steady despite the fear that clutched his heart. "O Cit Bolon Tum, great healer, guide my hands and heart. Grant me the wisdom to conquer this plague that besieges your people."

The jungle fell silent as a presence, both ancient and nurturing, filled the air. Cit Bolon Tum manifested before Kinich, not as a towering deity of might, but as a humble healer, his eyes filled with compassion. "Kinich, your devotion has pierced the veil of the heavens. The illness that plagues your city is born of the earth, a sickness that feeds on the imbalance of the natural world."

With a wave of his hand, Cit Bolon Tum revealed to Kinich the source of the fever—a rare herb that grew only in the shadow of the great Witz, the sacred mountains. "Seek this herb at dawn, when the world is bathed in the first light. Its power, combined with your knowledge, will break the fever's hold over your people."

Armed with Cit Bolon Tum's wisdom, Kinich embarked on his quest. As the first rays of dawn touched the peaks of the Witz, he found the herb, its leaves glistening with dew. With haste, he returned to Kan, where he prepared a remedy that was administered to Ahau Ixik and those afflicted by the fever.

Within days, the fever abated, and the city of Kan rejoiced. Ahau Ixik, restored to health, declared a feast in Kinich's honor, praising his devotion and skill. But Kinich knew the true hero of this tale was Cit Bolon Tum, whose guidance had saved not just the life of a ruler but the future of an entire city.

From that day forth, Kinich dedicated himself to maintaining the balance of the natural world, understanding that the health of his people was intricately tied to the health of the earth itself. And in the heart of the jungle, near the sacred cenote, a new temple was erected in honor of Cit Bolon Tum, a testament to the god's mercy and the healing power of faith.

[CHAPTER 20] — COLEL CAB

Amid the verdant embrace of the rainforest that cradles Yaxchilán, where the Usumacinta River whispers ancient secrets, there lived a beekeeper named Xunan. In a land where every blossom tells a story and every hum in the air carries the breath of the divine, Xunan's bees were her connection to the natural world, her cherished companions in the dance of life.

Xunan's devotion to her bees transcended mere care; it was a sacred bond, nurtured through rituals and offerings to Colel Cab, the revered goddess of bees. Her hives thrived, a testament to her faith and the goddess's favor, producing honey so golden and sweet it seemed a drop of the sun's own essence.

Yet, as the seasons turned, a shadow fell upon Yaxchilán. A blight, unseen and unforgiving, crept through the forest, wilting flowers and silencing the buzz of the bees. Xunan watched, heart heavy, as her hives languished, the once vibrant hum dwindling to a mournful silence. Desperate, she turned to Colel Cab, offering prayers and precious jade, pleading for her intervention.

One night, under a sky heavy with stars, Colel Cab answered. She appeared before Xunan, not as a fearsome deity, but as a figure cloaked in the gentle darkness of the jungle, her presence both awe-inspiring and comforting. Her voice, when she spoke, was the soft buzz of wings, the whisper of wind through the trees.

"Xunan, faithful servant of the hives, your devotion has reached my ears," Colel Cab intoned. "But understand this, the balance of life is delicate, as fragile as the wings of a bee. The blight is but a part of this balance, a test of faith and resilience."

Xunan, her spirit bolstered by the goddess's presence, found the courage to speak. "Great Colel Cab, I beg of you, show me the way to restore the balance, to heal the land and save my bees."

Colel Cab regarded her, a depth of wisdom in her gaze. "The answer lies not in the heavens but in the heart of the earth. Seek out the cenote to the west, where the waters touch the roots of the world. There, you will find what you seek."

With a resolve born of divine guidance, Xunan embarked on her journey, navigating the dense tapestry of the jungle, her path lit by the luminescent eyes of its nocturnal creatures. The cenote, hidden away like a gem in the forest's embrace, gleamed under the moonlight, its waters clear and deep.

Xunan dove, her body embraced by the cool liquid, descending into the heart of the cenote. Below, among the roots that drank from its waters, she found a cluster of flowers, untouched by the blight, their petals glowing with an ethereal light. She understood then that these were the key, a gift from Colel Cab herself.

Returning to Yaxchilán, Xunan infused her hives with the essence of these celestial flowers. Slowly, life returned to her garden, the bees awakening as if from a deep slumber, their hum once more a vibrant chorus in the symphony of the forest.

Colel Cab, watching from the shadows, saw the renewal of life, the balance restored through the perseverance and faith of a single devoted heart. And Xunan, her bond with the goddess of bees forever deepened, continued her work, a guardian of the sacred dance between the blossoms and the bees, under the watchful eyes of Colel Cab, whose presence in the hum of the hives whispered of the delicate balance of life, of death, and of rebirth.

[CHAPTER 21] — EK CHUAH

Through the dense, verdant canopy that blankets the land between Calakmul and Tikal, a merchant named Kukumatz weaved his way, his burden a cache of precious cacao, the food of the gods, destined for the great city's markets. In Mesoamerica, cacao was more than a mere commodity; it was a symbol of wealth, a medium of exchange, and an offering to the divine, integral to the very fabric of Mayan culture. Kukumatz, a devout follower of Ek Chuah, undertook his journey with a fervor that matched his faith, believing the protection of the god of merchants and war would shield him and his precious cargo.

Each year, before embarking on his trade route, Kukumatz performed a ritual sacrifice in honor of Ek Chuah, offering a cacao-colored dog to ensure his journeys were marked by success and safety. This year was no exception. Before leaving Calakmul, he had conducted the sacred rite, his heart heavy with the gravity of the sacrifice but buoyed by the certainty of divine oversight.

Kukumatz navigated the ancient trade paths, with his thoughts often drifting to the origins of chocolate, a secret entrusted to the Maya by the gods themselves. He marveled at how the bitter beans, when fermented, dried, roasted, and ground, transformed into a paste that became the heart of countless rituals and celebrations, a testament to the ingenuity of his people and the benevolence of deities like Ek Chuah.

As Kukumatz ventured through the dense underbrush that connected the great cities of Calakmul and Tikal, his path, shadowed by the towering ceiba trees, was laden with the promise of peril. The cacao beans he carried were not merely trade goods but symbols of wealth and divine connection, dedicated to Ek Chuah, the revered god of merchants and war. Aware of the dangers, Kukumatz's heart was steadfast, bolstered by his unwavering devotion and the rituals he performed in honor of Ek Chuah, including the annual sacrifice that sought the god's favor and protection.

His journey, however, was soon interrupted by the ominous presence of bandits, their eyes alight with the greed for the precious cargo. The tension in the air was palpable, a storm brewing on the horizon of fate. Yet, as they advanced, the air around Kukumatz shimmered, and Ek Chuah materialized, a towering figure of might and majesty, his warrior's eyes marked by the ominous black stripe and his presence commanding the awe and terror befitting a deity of his stature. "Who dares threaten my devotee?" Ek Chuah's voice thundered, a sound that echoed the clash of obsidian weapons.

There was no time for mercy, no room for clemency in Ek Chuah's realm of judgment. With a swift motion that mirrored the sudden onslaught of a tropical storm, Ek Chuah struck down the bandits, his divine power manifesting as a force as potent and unforgiving as the wars he presided over. The ground itself seemed to tremble under the weight of his wrath, a stark reminder of the consequences that befell those who dared to challenge or harm his devotees.

The forest, once filled with the tension of impending conflict, now lay silent, save for the soft murmur of the leaves whispering tales of divine retribution. Ek Chuah turned his formidable gaze upon Kukumatz, the fierceness melting away to reveal a semblance of divine benevolence. "Kukumatz, your faith has summoned my protection," he intoned, his voice echoing the depth of ancient wisdom. "Continue your journey with no fear, for I walk beside you."

EKukumatz, awestruck by the god's intervention, felt a renewed sense of purpose and determination. With Ek Chuah's blessing, he knew no harm would befall him. The journey to Tikal was completed without further incident, the cacao beans he carried now infused with the tales of divine protection and the power of unwavering faith.

Upon his return to Calakmul, the tale of Ek Chuah's intervention spread like wildfire, a story that would be etched in the memory of the city's inhabitants for generations to come. Kukumatz's experience served not only as a testament to the protective embrace of Ek Chuah for those who serve him with devotion but also as a stark reminder of the deity's might and the fate that awaits those who dare to cross his followers.

[CHAPTER 22] — HUNAB KU

In the vibrant heart of Puerto Vallarta, where the modern pulse of life intermingles with ancient spirits, lived a New Age seeker named Marisol. Drawn to the mystic lore of the Mayans, Marisol found a particular resonance with Hunab Ku, the creator god, whose philosophy of unity and balance mirrored her own quest for spiritual connection and understanding in a world that often seemed fragmented.

Marisol's journey into the teachings of Hunab Ku began under the vast canopy of the night sky, where the stars above Puerto Vallarta shone with a clarity that seemed to whisper of deeper mysteries. It was here, amidst the timeless dance of celestial bodies, that Marisol felt the presence of Hunab Ku, not as a deity to be feared, but as a guiding force, an essence that pervaded all existence, from the smallest grain of sand to the expansive universe itself.

Inspired by Hunab Ku's symbolism—a square within a circle, representing the harmony of opposites and the cycle of life—Marisol embarked on a personal mission to embody these principles in her daily life. She organized gatherings on the beaches of Puerto Vallarta, inviting others to join her in meditation and discussion, creating a community united in the pursuit of balance and universal love.

One evening, as Marisol and her companions sat in a circle on the soft sand, the air around them began to shimmer with an energy that defied explanation. In the center of their circle, the symbol of Hunab Ku appeared, etched in light against the darkness, pulsating with the heartbeat of the universe. A voice, as vast as the night sky, yet as intimate as a whispered secret, filled the space around them.

"Children of the stars," it began, "you have sought connection, understanding, and harmony, the very essence of my being. Know that the universe is a tapestry of interconnected threads, each life, each action woven into the fabric of existence. To honor me is to honor the unity of all things, to recognize the divine spark within each of you and to act as stewards of balance and love."

Marisol, awestruck by the manifestation of Hunab Ku's presence, felt a profound sense of peace and purpose. The gathering became a sacred moment, a bridge between the ancient world of the Mayans and the contemporary quest for spiritual fulfillment.

In the days that followed, Marisol's gatherings grew in number and spirit. The beaches of Puerto Vallarta became a sanctuary for those seeking solace and connection, a testament to the enduring power of Hunab Ku's message. Marisol, once a solitary seeker, became a beacon of light, guiding others on their journey towards unity and balance.

And so, in the bustling modernity of Puerto Vallarta, the ancient spirit of Hunab Ku found new expression, a reminder that the wisdom of the past holds keys to the challenges of the present. Through Marisol and her community, the teachings of Hunab Ku—of harmony, balance, and universal love—rippled out into the world, a legacy reborn under the watchful eyes of the stars.

[CHAPTER 23] — HUN-HUNAHPU AND VUCUB-HUNAHPU

In the verdant realms of the Mayan cosmos, where the fabric of reality was woven with the threads of divine will and mortal endeavor, there lived two brothers, Hun-Hunahpu and Vucub-Hunahpu. Sons of the creator gods, they inherited a world vibrant with the mystery and majesty of creation, a world where the whispers of the ancients echoed through the dense jungles and the stars told tales of timeless battles.

The brothers shared an unparalleled prowess in the ball game, an endeavor that was more than mere sport—it was a sacred act, a reflection of the cosmic dance between light and shadow, life and death. Their games, filled with the thud of the rubber ball and the cheers of the celestial audience, reverberated through the heavens and the earth, a testament to their skill and passion.

But beneath the realm of the living, in the dark bowels of Xibalba, the underworld's lords stirred with resentment. The noise of the brothers' games disturbed their sinister tranquility, a challenge to their authority and an affront to their pride. Thus, the lords of Xibalba, cunning and cruel, devised a plot to ensnare Hun-

Hunahpu and Vucub-Hunahpu, to bring them into their domain where the light of the sun dared not reach.

One fateful day, as the brothers reveled in the joy of their game, a messenger from Xibalba arrived, bearing an invitation—or rather, a challenge—from the underworld's rulers. "Great lords of the ball game," the messenger spoke with a voice as cold as the cenotes' depths, "the masters of Xibalba summon you to play upon their court, to test your mettle against the shadows."

The brothers, confident in their skill and intrigued by the challenge, accepted the invitation, unaware of the treachery that awaited them. "We shall play your game and triumph," Hun-Hunahpu declared, his voice brimming with the courage that defined him.

Upon their arrival in Xibalba, the brothers were met with trials designed to humiliate and defeat them. They navigated the treacherous paths laid before them, facing the House of Gloom, where darkness sought to swallow their resolve, and the House of Cold, which tried to freeze the warmth in their hearts.

Yet, it was in the ball court of Xibalba that the ultimate deception unfolded. Yet, the underworld was a realm where the gods' whims shaped reality, and the lords of Xibalba played by no rules but their own. The lords of the underworld, fearing the brothers' might, resorted to trickery, replacing the ball with a sphere of burning pitch.

In this game of shadows, Hun-Hunahpu and Vucub-Hunahpu played with all their might, their every move a defiance against the tyranny of Xibalba. But the game was rigged, the outcome preordained by the lords' treachery. In the end, the brothers were defeated, not by lack of skill, but by the deceit of their adversaries.

Vucub-Hunahpu's fate was sealed as well, bound to the shadowy realm, a victim of the lords' vengeance. Yet, even in death, Hun-Hunahpu's story was far from over. Hun-Hunahpu was decapitated, his head placed atop a calabash tree as a trophy and a warning to those who would dare challenge the darkness of Xibalba. His legacy, like the ball that he so masterfully played, would rebound through the annals of time, giving rise to new heroes, new battles, and the eternal cycle of life, death, and rebirth. His spirit, ensconced within the calabash tree, awaited the moment of its next ascension, a testament to the resilience of light in the face of overwhelming darkness.

[CHAPTER 24] — ITZAMNA

In the sacred city of Itzamal, where the stones themselves seemed to pulse with the wisdom of ages, there lived a scribe named Ahuil, whose life was dedicated to the study of time and the cosmos. His greatest aspiration was to understand the intricate calendar system, a marvel of mathematical and astronomical precision that governed the Mayan world. This system, a gift from Itzamna, the creator god, was not just a way to mark the passage of days but a profound expression of the divine order that structured the universe.

Itzamna, revered as the bringer of knowledge and the architect of the cosmos, had descended upon Itzamal in the days of antiquity. With a countenance as ancient as the stars and wisdom as deep as the cenotes, he had imparted the secrets of the calendar to the Maya, a system so advanced it included the concept of zero, a notion unparalleled in its time. The pyramids of Itzamal, with their 91 steps on each of the four sides, culminated in the final platform at the top, together symbolizing the 365 days of the solar year, a testament to Itzamna's mastery over time itself.

One night, as Ahuil labored by the light of a flickering torch, pouring over codices and charts, the air in his chamber grew thick, charged with a presence that stilled his very breath. Itzamna appeared before him, not as the fearsome deity of legend, but as a venerable old man, his eyes twinkling with celestial knowledge, his headdress a twin-headed serpent that seemed to whisper secrets of the universe.

"Ahuil, devoted seeker of the mysteries of time," Itzamna spoke, his voice the sound of rustling leaves. "Your dedication has pierced the veil between the earthly and the divine. What is it you seek?"

Overcome with awe, Ahuil found the courage to speak. "Great Itzamna, I wish to understand the full depth of your calendar, to grasp the cycles of time that you have laid out for us, that I might better serve my people and honor the gods."

Itzamna nodded, a smile playing upon his lips. "The calendar is more than numbers and cycles; it is the heartbeat of the universe, the breath of the cosmos. Each day is a step in the eternal dance of time, each cycle a story in the saga of creation. To truly understand, you must see as the gods see."

With a wave of his hand, Itzamna opened Ahuil's eyes to the cosmos. The scribe saw the movements of the planets and stars, the weaving of time and space, the divine order that underpinned all of creation. He saw how the concept of zero, a void from which all begins and to which all returns, was central to understanding the cycles of existence.

As Ahuil's vision of the cosmos began to fade, Itzamna's presence remained, a comforting and wise figure amidst the shadows of the chamber. "Ahuil, you have witnessed the dance of the cosmos, the eternal cycle that governs all existence. Now, let me bestow upon you the knowledge of the Long Count calendar, a gift of time that stretches beyond the horizon of human understanding," Itzamna spoke, his voice echoing the rhythm of the universe.

"The Long Count is a lattice of time, woven from the fabric of the cosmos. It measures the passage of days in units called 'baktuns,' each spanning approximately 394 years. Twenty baktuns complete a cycle, a span that reflects the rebirth and renewal of the world. This calendar is not just a measure of time but a map of destiny, charting the ebb and flow of the cosmic tides. It teaches us that time is a circle, ever returning, ever renewing, mirroring the cycle of creation and dissolution that defines the universe."

Ahuil listened, his mind alight with wonder and reverence. "Great Itzamna, how are we to use this profound knowledge?" he asked, humbled by the magnitude of the gift bestowed upon him.

"It is for you, and those who come after you, to keep the records, to mark the passage of the baktuns, and to observe the signs of change," Itzamna replied. "The Long Count calendar is a beacon for humanity, guiding your people through the ages, reminding them of their place within the grand tapestry of time. Through it, you will understand that every ending heralds a new beginning, that death is but a doorway to rebirth. Let this knowledge illuminate your path, and share it wisely with your kin."

With those final words, Itzamna's form dissolved into the night, leaving behind a trail of stardust that lingered in the air. Ahuil, now a guardian of one of the greatest treasures of Mayan civilization, dedicated his life to the study and teaching of the Long Count calendar. Through his efforts, and those of the scribes and astronomers who followed, the wisdom of the Long Count illuminated the Mayan understanding of time, reinforcing their connection to the cosmos and to the divine cycles of birth, death, and renewal.

The legacy of Itzamna, through Ahuil, continued to shape the Mayan world, a reminder of the unity between the divine and the mortal, the celestial and the earthly. And in Itzamal and other Mayan cities, the steps of the pyramids stood as a silent homage to Itzamna, the god who had mastered time, who had sown the seeds of knowledge and watched as they blossomed into a civilization that reached for the stars.

[CHAPTER 25] — IXCHEL

In the verdant lands that surround Quirigua, where the Copán River nourishes the earth and the whispers of the ancestors still echo through the dense canopy, there lived a midwife named Nicté-Ha. Known throughout the city for her wisdom and compassion, Nicté-Ha was a devoted servant of Ixchel, the moon goddess of fertility and childbirth. Her hut, adorned with symbols of Ixchel—a serpent for wisdom and a rabbit for fertility— stood as a beacon of hope for all expectant mothers in the region.

Nicté-Ha's dedication to Ixchel went beyond mere admiration; it was a profound connection that guided her in her sacred duty. She believed that within each birth, the touch of Ixchel's hand could be felt, guiding and protecting both mother and child through the perilous journey of childbirth. It was this belief that led Nicté-Ha to the ancient temple of Ixchel in Quirigua on the eve of the most challenging delivery she had ever faced.

Under the silver glow of the full moon, Nicté-Ha knelt before the stone effigy of Ixchel, her heart heavy with the burden of the task ahead. "Great Ixchel," she prayed, "guardian of women and bringer of life, lend me your strength, for I fear the child will not come into this world without your divine intervention."

As the words left her lips, the air around Nicté-Ha shimmered with a gentle radiance, and Ixchel appeared before her, not as an imposing deity, but as a comforting presence, her eyes filled with the infinite compassion of a thousand generations. "Nicté-Ha," the goddess spoke, her voice the soothing sound of rain on leaves, "your faith has called me forth. You shall not face this trial alone, for the lives of those you aid are precious to me."

Empowered by Ixchel's blessing, Nicté-Ha returned to the expectant mother's side, her hands steady and her spirit unbreakable. The night was long, and the labor arduous, but Nicté-Ha felt an unseen force guiding her actions, soothing the pain of the mother and easing the passage of the child into the world.

As dawn broke and the first cries of the newborn pierced the quiet of the early morning, Nicté-Ha knew that Ixchel had been with them throughout the night. The child was healthy, and the mother, though exhausted, was filled with joy. Word of the miraculous birth spread through Quirigua, reinforcing the people's faith in Ixchel and the sacred bond between the goddess and the midwives who served her.

Nicté-Ha, her reputation as a gifted midwife now intertwined with the divine favor of Ixchel, continued her work with renewed vigor. She taught the women of Quirigua the wisdom of Ixchel, from the healing properties of herbs to the sacred rituals that honored the cycles of life. And in every birth she attended, the presence of Ixchel was felt, a testament to the enduring power of faith and the unbreakable chain of life that binds all generations.

[CHAPTER 26] — IXMUCANÉ AND IXPIYACOC

In the aftermath of creation, as the world crafted by Bitol began to flourish with life's myriad forms, the divine assembly convened to discuss the fate of this new world. Among them, Ajbit sought the wisdom of Ixmucané and Ixpiyacoc, the venerable sages whose insight had guided the cosmos from time immemorial.

"A world of beauty and complexity unfolds before us," Ajbit began, his voice resonating with the weight of responsibility. "Yet, it yearns for beings who can appreciate its wonders, who can weave the threads of thought and emotion into the tapestry of existence."

Ixmucané, whose essence was as nurturing as the earth itself, shared her thoughts, her words infused with the depth of maternal wisdom. "The land and sea, the sky and stars, they all sing a song of unity and diversity. The beings we create must reflect this harmony, capable of understanding and reverence, of love and compassion."

Ixpiyacoc, whose eyes saw beyond the veil of the present into the realms of possibility, nodded in agreement. "They must be more than mere inhabitants of this world; they must be its stewards, guardians of the balance that sustains all life. But what form shall they take, and from what material shall we craft their essence?"

"I began with mud," Ajbit revealed, the disappointment palpable in his tone. "I envisioned beings molded from the earth itself, connected deeply to the land they would inhabit. Yet, they dissolved under the first rains, as fleeting as dreams at dawn."

Ixpiyacoc, his gaze piercing the veil of potentialities, responded, "The essence of life is resilience, Ajbit. Mud, while abundant and pliable, lacks the endurance to withstand the trials of existence. Look to materials that embody both the fluidity of life and the strength to persist."

Inspired, Ajbit turned to obsidian, its gleaming surface a mirror to the night sky. "From obsidian, I crafted beings of strength and beauty, yet they were inflexible, their spirits as impenetrable as the stone from which they were carved."

Ixmucané, her voice as soothing as the earth's embrace, suggested, "Balance, Ajbit. Creation thrives not just in strength but in the capacity for connection and change. Reflect on materials that marry durability with the warmth of life."

Ajbit, guided by the wisdom shared, shaped beings from wood, instilling in them the breath of life. "They moved and toiled, yet their essence was hollow, devoid of the spark that ignites passion and purpose."

Ixpiyacoc, contemplating the cycle of growth and decay, advised, "Life's essence is not merely to exist but to feel, to yearn, to aspire. Your creations must possess the spirit of the divine, a soul that seeks beyond mere survival."

With renewed resolve, Ajbit experimented with leaves, their ephemeral beauty a testament to life's transitory nature. "Their whispers were like music, yet they lacked the fortitude to endure, to leave a lasting legacy upon the earth."

Ixmucané, reflecting on the fleeting beauty of creation, counseled, "The dance of life requires a stage both vast and enduring. Seek a material that offers not just the beauty of the moment but the promise of tomorrow."

Ajbit's journey led him to clay, sculpting figures that bore the promise of permanence. "Yet, under the sun's gaze, they fissured and broke, their silence a heavy cloak that stifled the spirit within."

Ixpiyacoc, his vision clear, declared, "True creation weaves together the delicate and the resilient, the tangible and the ethereal. Your next attempt must embrace this duality, Ajbit. Consider the essence of life that cycles through death and rebirth."

It was in the golden embrace of maize that Ajbit found his answer. "Maize, with its endless cycles, became the vessel for my aspirations. In it, I discovered the harmony of existence—life, death, and the rebirth that follows."

Ixmucané and Ixpiyacoc, witnessing Ajbit's revelation, nodded in approval. "Maize embodies the principles of life itself," Ixmucané affirmed. "It sustains, it nurtures, and it returns to the earth to rise anew. Your creations, born of maize, will carry the essence of the cosmos within them, living testaments to the cycles that govern all."

Ixpiyacoc, inspired by the convergence of their insights, added, "These maize beings shall be our children, reflections of our highest aspirations. They will possess the capacity for wonder and the desire for knowledge, the ability to create and the wisdom to preserve."

Together, the divine trio set about the task of creation, their combined will shaping the maize dough into the first humans. As they worked, they imbued their creations with qualities essential for the fulfillment of their divine purpose—curiosity and empathy, strength and gentleness, courage and humility.

When the task was complete, the gods stood back to behold their work. The maize humans stirred to life, their eyes opening to the wonders of the world around them, their hearts filled with the spark of consciousness.

"These are our children," Ixmucané declared, a sense of pride and hope suffusing her words. "Through them, the beauty of creation will be known, and the balance of the cosmos upheld. They will sing the songs of the earth and stars, and in their voices, we will hear the echo of our own."

Ixpiyacoc, gazing upon the first humans with a visionary's eye, foresaw the challenges and triumphs that lay ahead. "They will journey through light and shadow, their paths fraught with trials. But in their hearts burns the flame of resilience, the light of our guidance. They are the culmination of our dreams, the bearers of our legacy."

And so, under the watchful eyes of their creators, the maize humans began their journey upon the earth, a journey that would weave their stories into the fabric of Mayan lore. Through them, the world created by Bitol would know joy and sorrow, hope and despair, love and loss— the full spectrum of existence.

After witnessing the creation of humanity and the birth of the maize beings, a profound sense of inspiration washed over Ixmucané and Ixpiyacoc. The world, vibrant with the lives of their creations, sparked within them a desire to contribute even more intimately to the tapestry of existence. In a union of wisdom and divinity, they decided to bring forth their own offspring into the world.

Their communion was one of deep spiritual and cosmic significance, a melding of divine essences that would result in the birth of two remarkable beings: Hun-Hunahpu and Vucub-Hunahpu. These sons, born of the celestial, were destined for greatness, imbued with the wisdom of their parents and a profound connection to the very fabric of creation.

As Hun-Hunahpu and Vucub-Hunahpu grew, they exhibited an extraordinary affinity for Pok-Ta-Pok, the sacred ball game that mirrored the celestial dance of the cosmos itself. Their prowess on the ball court was unmatched, a reflection of their divine heritage and a testament to the skills imparted by their parents. The brothers played not just for victory, but as a celebration of life, a homage to the cycles of existence that their family had so crucially shaped.

Their games became legendary, drawing spectators from across the realms, both mortal and divine. In the brothers, the people saw the embodiment of harmony and excellence, a bridge between the gods and humanity. Ixmucané and Ixpiyacoc watched their sons with pride, knowing that their legacy would resonate through the ages, a perpetual reminder of the power of creation, the beauty of life, and the enduring bond between the celestial and the earthly.

In Hun-Hunahpu and Vucub-Hunahpu, the story of creation found its champions, beings who would carry forward the wisdom and the spirit of their forebears. Through them, the narrative of the cosmos continued to unfold, a saga of challenge, triumph, and the eternal game of existence.

[CHAPTER 27] — IXTAB

In the verdant expanses surrounding Lamanai, where ancient pyramids touched the sky and the air hummed with the whispers of the past, there lived a builder named Chaak. His skill was unparalleled, his dedication to his craft a testament to the Mayan belief in the sanctity of creation. Chaak's structures were more than mere buildings; they were offerings to the gods, each stone a prayer set in mortar.

Tragedy struck one fateful day when a temple, newly erected under Chaak's watchful eye, crumbled during a sacred ceremony, claiming the life of a young acolyte. The sorrow of the loss was immeasurable, the weight of guilt unbearable. In Mayan society, the architect of a structure that failed bore a heavy burden, not just for the loss of life but for the perceived offense to the gods.

Chaak, heart heavy with grief and responsibility, found himself wandering the shadowed paths of the jungle, seeking solace from the torment that consumed him. He wrapped a rope around a Ceiba tree that grew near a cenote. He wrapped the other end around his neck. Then he leaped into the cenote, to end his grief and pay for his offense to the gods.

In the ethereal realm beyond the mortal coil, where the boundaries of earth and heaven blur into a tapestry of spiritual continuation, Ixtab waited with the patience of eternity. She, the guardian of souls who departed by their own hand, stood as a beacon of understanding and compassion amidst the celestial domain. Her presence was a solace, her embrace a passage to peace for those who sought release from their earthly burdens.

As Chaak's spirit transcended the terrestrial plane, leaving behind the trials that bound him to the material world, he found himself in a realm bathed in a gentle light, a stark contrast to the darkness he had known. Ixtab, with her serene countenance, was there to greet him, her visage devoid of judgment, only offering the unconditional acceptance that had eluded him in life.

"Welcome, Chaak," Ixtab's voice, soft as the whisper of leaves in the wind, enveloped him. "Your journey has been one of turmoil and strife, but here, you shall find solace. Your actions have led you to this sanctuary, a place where honor is bestowed upon those who have faced their end with the courage to seek freedom."

Around them, the paradise that Ixtab promised unfolded—a lush, verdant landscape where the sky shimmered with hues of twilight, eternal and soothing. Here, the spirits of warriors, women of childbirth, and those like Chaak mingled, their presence a tapestry of stories, each honored equally for the paths they chose and the battles they fought, be they on the battlefield, in the throes of labor, or within the recesses of their own minds.

"Here, you are freed from the burdens that weighed upon your shoulders," Ixtab continued, guiding Chaak into the heart of paradise. "Here, your spirit may heal, grow, and eventually, be reborn. For in this realm, every end is but a new beginning, and every soul is cherished for its journey."

Chaak, absorbing the tranquility and acceptance that permeated this realm, felt the first stirrings of peace in what felt like an eternity. The understanding that his departure from the physical world was not an end, but a transition into a new state of being, lifted the shadows that had clouded his existence.

In the company of Ixtab and the honored souls that shared this paradise, Chaak found a sense of belonging and purpose. He learned that every life, every choice, carried its own form of bravery, and in the eyes of Ixtab, every soul deserved a place of honor in the afterlife.

[CHAPTER 28] — IXCHUP

In the verdant lands that stretch towards the sea near Tulum, where the cliffs rise as guardians of timeless secrets, a group of Mayan children played under the watchful gaze of the sun. Their laughter mingled with the whispers of the wind, carrying their joy across the lush landscape that was their playground. Among these children was a girl named Kawayum, whose fascination with the colors of the world knew no bounds. She found wonder in the simplest of sights—the vibrant hues of flowers, the deep greens of the jungle, and most of all, the rare glimpses of rainbows that arched across the sky after a gentle rain.

Kawayum's curiosity about rainbows was insatiable. She questioned why they appeared and where they hid when the sun reclaimed the sky. Her grandmother, a wise keeper of tales, told her of Ixchup, the goddess of rainbows. Ixchup, considered to be a manifestation of Ixchel, was a deity as elusive as the phenomenon Kawayum adored. According to her grandmother, Ixchup painted the sky with her palette of colors as a bridge between the gods and the people of the earth, reminding them of the beauty and promise that followed the rain.

One day, after a morning shower that left the air fresh and the earth rich with the scent of life, Kawayum and her friends ventured to the top of a hill that overlooked the ocean. There, as if summoned by their presence, a magnificent rainbow appeared, more vivid and closer than any they had seen before. Kawayum, awestruck, whispered a wish to see Ixchup, to thank her for the gift of colors that brought so much joy.

As the words left her lips, a gentle breeze caressed the hilltop, and before the children stood Ixchup, a beautiful young woman, radiant and ethereal, with a rabbit by her feet. Her robes shimmered with all the colors of the rainbow; her smile as warm as the sun that fueled her canvas. "Kawayum," she spoke, her voice the melody of raindrops on leaves, "your appreciation for the beauty of the world has called me forth. The rainbows are a reminder of the wonders that exist around us, reflections of the light through water, yes, but also symbols of hope and connection."

Ixchup, with a gesture as graceful as the unfolding of a flower at dawn, drew the children closer. The air around them seemed to shimmer, as if the very essence of the rainbow had descended to envelop them in its embrace. "Each color you see in the rainbow," she began, her voice a gentle echo of distant thunder, "carries with it a story, a piece of the world's soul."

"Green," she continued, pointing to the vibrant band of color that seemed to resonate with the life force of the jungle surrounding Tulum, "is the heartbeat of the earth, the pulse of the forests and fields. It speaks of growth, of life unfurling from the soil, and of the eternal cycle of renewal."

Her gaze then lifted to the serene blue, mirroring the vastness of the sky above and the ocean's depths. "Blue is the breath of the sky and the sea, the expanse that teaches us about the infinite possibilities and the depths of our own hearts. It calls to the spirit of exploration and the peace that comes from knowing we are a part of something boundless."

Ixchup's eyes sparkled as they moved to the radiant red arc. "Red is the essence of fire, the transformative power that warms, illuminates, and changes. It is the passion within us, the force that drives us to create, to love, and to live fiercely."

She then touched the orange part of the spectrum, and the color seemed to glow more intensely. "Orange combines the energy of red with the joy of yellow. It is the hue of dawn, the promise of a new day, and the creativity that arises when we embrace change with enthusiasm."

Smiling, Ixchup caressed the yellow light. "Yellow is the sun's embrace, the warmth that nurtures and the clarity that illuminates our path. It represents the joy of being, the laughter of children, and the wisdom that lightens our burdens."

Her fingers traced the path to the indigo and violet, where the rainbow's colors deepened into mystery. "Indigo and violet are the colors of twilight and the deepening sky, where dreams and intuition dwell. Indigo invites us to look within, to the wisdom that comes from introspection and meditation. Violet connects us to the mystical, to the realms beyond our sight, reminding us that the universe is full of wonders yet to be understood."

Ixchup's gaze encompassed all the children before her. "The rainbow is a covenant of balance and harmony. Each color, a thread in the fabric of existence, woven together to remind us of the beauty that arises from unity and diversity. Look for rainbows, not just in the sky, but in each other, and remember the lessons they teach us about life, about the world, and about the beauty of coming together."

Ixchup's visit then coming near its end, she touched Kawayum's forehead gently. At that moment, Kawayum knew that she would always find joy in the simple wonders of the world, and that the rainbows would forever be a sign of the goddess's presence and the promise of beauty that follows the rain.

As Ixchup's form began to fade, leaving a soft glow in the air, the children found themselves alone once more, the memory of her words a treasure they would carry with them. In the days to come, they would share the stories of the rainbow's colors, spreading Ixchup's message of balance, beauty, and unity, a legacy of wonder that would illuminate their lives like a perpetual rainbow.

From that day on, whenever a rainbow arched across the skies of Tulum, Kawayum and her friends would remember their encounter with Ixchup, the goddess of rainbows. And Kawayum, in particular, carried the lesson of finding beauty in the aftermath, cherishing each color as a gift from the divine, a bridge between the heavens and the earth.

[CHAPTER 29] — IX TUB TUN

Deep within the verdant embrace of Altun Ha, a city resplendent with the achievements of the Maya, lived a jade artisan named Tzimin. His skill in shaping the stubborn rock into forms both delicate and divine was unrivaled, a gift he attributed to the grace of Ix Tub Tun, the goddess whose spirit dwelled within each vein of jade that coursed through the earth. In Maya belief, jade was the embodiment of the breath of life itself, its cool, verdant hues a reflection of the vibrant life force that animated the world.

Tzimin embarked on his most ambitious creation yet: a carved jade head of Kinich Ahau, the Sun God, meant to grace the inner sanctum of the city's grandest temple. This was not merely an offering of artistry; it was a conduit for the divine, a way to draw the gaze of the gods themselves to Altun Ha.

As Tzimin worked, chiseling and shaping the jade with hands guided by a reverence for Ix Tub Tun, whispers of the serpant goddess's voice echoed through the chambers of his mind. "Within this stone lies the heartbeat of the earth," she intoned, her words a melody that danced with the tapping of Tzimin's tools.

"Infuse this effigy with the reverence it deserves, for through it, the sun's eternal blaze will shine."

Nights turned to days, and days to nights, as Tzimin toiled, his vision and hands solely devoted to the manifestation of Kinich Ahau's likeness. The jade, tough and resistant at first, seemed to yield under his touch as if consenting to bear the image of the deity.

Upon completion, the jade head was not just a sculpture but a masterpiece imbued with the essence of life itself. Its eyes, polished to a gleaming finish, captured the first light of dawn, reflecting it back as if the sun god himself peered into the soul of Altun Ha.

The day arrived for the head's placement within the temple, a ceremony attended by the city's inhabitants, their hearts swelled with pride and awe. As the jade head was settled into its sacred niche, a beam of sunlight pierced the temple's aperture, illuminating the effigy in a halo of golden light. A collective gasp rose from the gathered crowd, a moment of unity and wonder shared by all.

But the story does not end with the setting of the stone. For Ix Tub Tun, pleased with Tzimin's devotion and craftsmanship, blessed Altun Ha with a prosperity previously unknown. The crops flourished as if kissed by Kinich Ahau himself, and the city became a beacon of abundance and artistry.

Tzimin, however, found his greatest reward in the silent communion with the jade, the medium through which he touched the divine. He continued his work, each piece a prayer, each stroke a hymn to Ix Tub Tun and the pantheon that watched over the Maya.

[CHAPTER 30] — IXQUIC

In the heart of the Mayan world, where the dense jungle whispered ancient secrets and the stars told tales of the gods, there was a princess named Ixquic, whose destiny was intertwined with the divine. Raised on the stories of her ancestors and the mysteries of the gods, Ixquic felt a pull towards a legend she had been cautioned against—a tree unlike any other, bearing not just fruit but a legacy of magic and power.

This was no ordinary tree. It had sprung from the remains of Hun-Hunahpu, the revered magician god, transforming his spirit into a guardian of knowledge and enchantment. Among its branches hung a skull, not a symbol of death but a vessel of divine wisdom.

Drawn by a force she could not explain, Ixquic ventured into the forbidden reaches of the jungle, guided by the stars and her own fearless heart. There, in a clearing bathed in moonlight, stood the tree, its presence commanding and ethereal, bearing no fruit but the head of a god. The skull of Hun-Hunahpu, still possessing the spark of divine mischief, spoke to her. "Reach out your hand," it urged.

With reverence, Ixquic extended her hand, accepting the offering. In that moment, it spat into her palm, a miraculous conception that defied the laws of mortals and gods alike, bound her to a fate both wondrous and daunting — she would bear the hero twins, warriors of light destined to challenge the darkness.

Yet, her path was fraught with peril. The lords of Xibalba, enraged by her defiance and the promise she carried, decreed her death and sent owls to bring back her heart. Ixquic, her spirit as indomitable as the heroes she would mother, pleaded with the owls, the hunters of the night, for mercy.

"Let me live," she implored, "not for my sake, but for the future that grows within me. The sons I bear will be the dawn that Xibalba cannot extinguish."

Moved by her plea, the owls conspired to deceive the lords of the underworld. They took a pomegranate, its interior carved to mimic a heart, as proof of their deed, allowing Ixquic to flee to the realm above.

There, in the embrace of Ixmukané, the mother of Hun-Hunahpu, Ixquic found sanctuary. She nurtured the life within her, and in time, gave birth to Xbalanque and

Hunahpú, the luminaries who would become the moon and the sun.

Ixquic's tale, woven into the fabric of the Mayan cosmos, is a testament to the power of faith, the resilience of the spirit, and the eternal cycle of renewal. Her journey from the shadows of Xibalba to the light of creation is a reminder of the strength that lies in the heart of all women, a strength capable of overcoming darkness and birthing new dawns.

[CHAPTER 31] — JACAWITZ

Amid the misty highlands that cradle Q'umarkaj, where the mountains whisper secrets of old, lived a young farmer named Xanil. His days were spent tending to maize and beans under the watchful eyes of the surrounding peaks, guardians of his people's prosperity and woe. Xanil, though humble in speech, harbored a deep reverence for the land that sustained them, often leaving offerings of jade and woven fabrics at the altars dotting the landscape, hoping to appease the spirits dwelling within.

One evening, as the sun dipped below the horizon, painting the sky in hues of orange and purple, the ground beneath Xanil's feet trembled. From the heart of the mountain, a figure emerged, cloaked in the red glow of molten rock, eyes burning with the fires of the earth's core. It was Jacawitz, the mountain god, whose presence was both a blessing and a harbinger of the raw power that lay beneath.

"Xanil," boomed Jacawitz, his voice echoing off the mountain walls, "you have honored the land, but your people have forgotten the might of those who dwell within it. They take from the earth, giving nothing in return, stripping away its bounty without a thought for the morrow."

Terror gripped Xanil's heart, yet he stood firm, his respect for the deity before him overshadowing his fear. "Great Jacawitz, we have strayed from the old ways, lost in the ebb and flow of time. What can be done to restore the balance, to show our respect for your strength and generosity?"

Jacawitz's gaze softened, the fiery glow in his eyes dimming to embers. "Teach your people to see not just the soil, but the life it holds. Let them understand that each mountain, each stone, is alive with my essence. They must learn to give, not just take, to live in harmony with the land that cradles them."

With a rumble that seemed to carry the weight of the earth, Jacawitz melded back into the mountain, leaving Xanil alone under the stars. The young farmer knew what he must do. Day by day, he spoke to his neighbors, sharing the words of Jacawitz, teaching them to see the mountains not as mere rock, but as living entities deserving of respect and care.

In time, the people of Q'umarkaj began to change their ways. They planted trees to hold the soil, conserved water, and made offerings to Jacawitz, acknowledging his dominion over the land. The earthquakes that once threatened their city became less frequent, and the harvests grew more bountiful.

[CHAPTER 32] — JURAKAN

Amid the verdant highlands where Iximche stood, a city of profound spiritual significance, there lived a man named Votan. Votan was not of noble blood, nor was he graced with the wealth of traders. His wealth lay in the soil, tending to his crops with a devotion that bordered on reverence. In a land where the whims of the gods could dictate the bounty of the next harvest, Votan's faith was his bulwark against the capricious nature of fate.

It was during the season of planting that the skies above Iximche began to darken, not with the promising clouds of nourishing rains but with the ominous shadow of Jurakan, the god of storms. His arrival was not heralded by the gentle pattering of life-giving water but by the roar of thunder and the sharp spears of lightning, tearing the heavens asunder.

Votan, aware of the impending tempest, stood resolute in his fields, his eyes fixed upon the gathering maelstrom. It was then that Jurakan descended, his form as tumultuous as the storms he wielded. "Why do you stand before me, mortal?" Jurakan's voice boomed, a sound that echoed the thunderclaps that accompanied his presence.

"I stand for my crops, for my family, and for the people of Iximche," Votan replied, his voice steady despite the swirling chaos. "I beseech you, spare us your fury. Let the rains nourish the earth, not destroy it."

Jurakan, taken aback by the mortal's audacity, narrowed his eyes, a flash of lightning illuminating his features— features that bore the marks of countless storms, his eyes deep pools of shifting shadows. "You dare to ask this of me, to command the storm itself?"

"Not command, O mighty Jurakan, but to plead for mercy, for balance. Let your rains fall, but let them be a blessing, not a curse."

A silence fell between them, punctuated only by the distant rumble of thunder. Jurakan, the embodiment of nature's tempestuous might, contemplated the farmer's words. In Votan's plea, he sensed not the cowardice of a man afraid of the storm's wrath but the courage of one who respects the forces that shape the world.

"Very well," Jurakan conceded, his voice softening like the distant rumble of a passing storm. "Your words have moved me, Votan of Iximche. The rains will come, but they will bring life, not destruction."

True to his word, Jurakan lifted his arms, and the skies responded. The violent winds abated, the lightning ceased its dance, and in their place came a gentle rain, a cascade of droplets that kissed the earth, coaxing life from the soil. Votan watched in awe as the god of storms tamed the tempest, transforming fury into fertility.

As Jurakan ascended, leaving behind the promise of a bountiful harvest, Votan knew that the balance between mankind and the divine was a delicate one, sustained by respect, faith, and the occasional audacity to speak from the heart. Iximche would thrive, its people nourished by the bounty Jurakan's rains promised, a testament to the day when a simple farmer stood before a god and pleaded for the future.

[CHAPTER 33] — KINICH AHAU

In the golden embrace of Uxmal, where stone pyramids catch the first light of dawn, there lived a poet named Pakal. Unlike the warriors and kings celebrated in grand epics, Pakal's battles were fought with words, his victories won in the hearts of those who heard his verses. In a world where the gods walked among the mortals, Pakal sought to capture the essence of the divine in his poetry, to bridge the celestial with the earthly through his craft.

It was during the zenith of the dry season, when the sun scorched the earth with its unyielding gaze, that Pakal found himself wandering the city's outskirts, parched and weary, yet driven by an insatiable desire for inspiration. It was then that Kinich Ahau, the sun god himself, descended before Pakal, cloaked in the brilliance of the midday sun, his presence a palpable heat that shimmered in the air.

"Why do you wander the lands of my dominion, poet of Uxmal?" Kinich Ahau's voice was a melody, the cadence of which held the power of the sun's rays—warm, life-giving, yet formidable.

"I seek the words to paint your portrait, O luminous Kinich Ahau," Pakal replied, his voice steady despite the awe that filled him. "I wish to compose a poem that might capture a fraction of your splendor, to share your light with those who dwell in shadow."

The sun god regarded Pakal, a spark of interest lighting in his ancient eyes. "Very well," he decreed, "I shall grant you a glimpse of my essence. But know this, mortal: the true measure of a god cannot be captured in mere words."

With a gesture from Kinich Ahau, the world around Pakal transformed. He witnessed the birth of dawn, the sun's rays chasing away the night's embrace; he felt the noonday heat, the lifeblood of the earth; he basked in the gentle warmth of the setting sun, a promise of rest and renewal. Each moment, a symphony of light and shadow, played before Pakal's eyes, a testament to Kinich Ahau's eternal cycle.

When the vision faded, Pakal found himself alone once more, the encounter with the sun god seared into his memory. With a heart aflame with inspiration, he returned to Uxmal, where he composed a poem that sought to encapsulate the divine spectacle he had witnessed:

Beneath the gaze of Kinich Ahau,
where light unfurls across Uxmal's stone,
a poet walks, heart open, seeking
the essence of day.

In the silence of dawn,
where shadows retreat and the world holds its breath,
there, in the softness of first light,
the sun whispers secrets
old as time.

Midday arrives, bold and unyielding,
the zenith of Kinich Ahau's arc,
a testament to power, to life given and sustained,
a realm where every leaf, every stone
basks in divine attention.

As the day leans into evening,
colors bleed into the sky—
a canvas of golds, of reds, a painter's last stroke,
the sun god's gentle nod towards night,
a cycle, endless, revered.

This is Kinich Ahau,
not just deity of the high sun,
but guardian of moments fleeting,

of warmth that fades into cool shadows,
of light that promises to return
after the world has turned in sleep.

In every sunrise, hope is reborn,
in every sunset, peace is whispered,
and in the heart of the poet,
words strive to mirror
the beauty of a god's journey across the sky,
never quite capturing,
always in awe.

Pakal's poem spread throughout Uxmal and beyond, a tribute to the sun god's majesty and the poet's skill. Yet, Pakal himself knew that his verses were but shadows of the true wonder of Kinich Ahau. In seeking to capture the divine, he had found a deeper appreciation for the mysteries that lay beyond the realm of words. And in his heart, a new verse began to form, a never-ending ode to the dance of light and life.

[CHAPTER 34] — KINICH KAKMO

In the luminous city of Izamal, where the golden hues of the sun painted every stone and street, there lived a salt maker named Naal. His trade was one of patience and precision, harnessing the power of the sun to transform the brine of the sea into crystals of salt. This salt was not merely for seasoning but a precious commodity, essential for the preservation of food and an integral part of rituals and offerings.

Naal's work connected him deeply to the cycles of nature, to the ebb and flow of tides, and to the relentless journey of the sun across the sky. Yet, in his heart, there was a yearning for something beyond the tangible, a desire to touch the divine essence that fueled his daily toil. It was this yearning that drew the gaze of Kinich Kakmo, the Great Sun-Faced Fire Macaw, whose spirit watched over Izamal and its inhabitants.

One day, as the sun reached its zenith and Naal tended to his salt pans, the air around him shimmered with heat, and from this mirage emerged Kinich Kakmo, not in the imposing form of a deity, but as a macaw of radiant plumage, each feather a flame, each glance a ray of light. Naal, struck by the sight, fell to his knees, for he knew before him stood a god.

"Why do you labor under my gaze, salt maker?" Kinich Kakmo asked, his voice a melody that resonated with the warmth of the midday sun.

Naal lifted his eyes, finding courage in the presence of the divine. "Great Kinich Kakmo, I seek to capture your essence, to preserve the vitality of the sun within the salt I harvest, that it may bring sustenance and purity to the people of Izamal."

The macaw tilted his head, considering the mortal before him. "Your task is noble, and your spirit is pure. The salt you craft is a vessel of life, much like the rays I bestow upon the earth. Let me show you the true power of the sun."

With a beat of his fiery wings, Kinich Kakmo took to the sky, circling above the salt pans. As he flew, the waters below began to simmer, then boil, under an intense heat that was both fearsome and magnificent. Naal watched in awe as, before his eyes, the brine transformed, crystallizing into salt of unparalleled purity and brilliance.

"Your salt shall carry the essence of the sun, Naal," Kinich Kakmo proclaimed, descending once more to the earth. "Let it be a reminder of the balance between the elements, of the harmony between the divine and the mortal. But remember, the gift of the sun is one of creation and destruction alike. Use it wisely, for it holds the power to sustain life and to take it away."

As the deity vanished, leaving behind only the lingering warmth of his presence, Naal knew his life's work had been forever changed. The salt he would henceforth produce carried not just the taste of the sea but the energy of the sun, a sacred bond between earth and sky, mortal and divine.

From that day forth, the salt of Izamal was sought after far and wide, not just for its flavor but for its vitality. And Naal, the humble salt maker, became a guardian of a divine gift, his craft a testament to the day the Sun-Faced Fire Macaw revealed the true essence of the sun.

[CHAPTER 35] — KUKULKAN

Beneath the azure skies of Chichen Itzá, where the pyramids pierce the heavens and the sacred cenotes mirror the underworld, there walked a weaver named Tihax. In a city that thrived on the divine, where every stone and carving whispered of gods and legends, Tihax's life was a tapestry of colors, each thread a story, each pattern a prayer. Yet, in his heart, there was a longing, a desire to understand the mysteries that the gods wove into the fabric of the world.

It was during the zenith of the equinox, when the shadow of the great pyramid of Kukulcan slithered like a serpent made of darkness, that Tihax's life would intertwine with the divine. As the city gathered to witness the descent of Kukulkan, the feathered serpent god, Tihax stood apart, his eyes not on the pyramid but on the horizon, where the sky kissed the earth.

Suddenly, the air around him shimmered, and before him appeared Kukulkan, not as a towering deity but as a serpent adorned with feathers of unimaginable colors, each hue a testament to the god's dominion over the earth and sky. Tihax fell to his knees, overcome by the god's presence, but Kukulkan spoke in a voice that was a gentle hiss, "Rise, Tihax of Chichen Itzá. Why do you seek the horizon when the divine descends before you?"

Tihax, emboldened by the god's question, replied, "Great Kukulkan, I seek not just to witness the divine but to understand it, to weave your essence into the tapestry of humanity."

Kukulkan, intrigued by the weaver's ambition, uncoiled and moved closer. "Understanding the divine is no simple task, Tihax. It requires more than sight; it demands insight. Will you journey with me, to see the world through the eyes of a god?"

With a nod, Tihax accepted, and in an instant, they were lifted into the sky, the world below unfolding like a vast tapestry. They soared over mountains and valleys, rivers and forests, each landscape a different stitch in the earth's design. Kukulkan showed Tihax the delicate balance of nature, the cycle of life and death, and the interconnectedness of all things.

As they traveled, Kukulkan shared his wisdom, each word a thread in the intricate weave of creation. "To understand the divine, one must see the beauty in the mundane, the sacred in the profane, and the eternal in the ephemeral."

When they returned to Chichen Itzá, Tihax saw the city anew, each stone a symbol, each shadow a story. With a heart full of gratitude, Tihax set to work, his hands weaving not just cloth but a narrative of divine complexity.

The tapestry he created was unlike any other, a masterpiece that captured the essence of Kukulkan, the feathered serpent god. It depicted the balance of the cosmos, the cycle of the seasons, and the unity of earth and sky. And at its center was Kukulkan, a bridge between the mortal and the divine, his feathers a spectrum of colors that danced in the light.

When the people of Chichen Itzá beheld the tapestry, they were awestruck, for through Tihax's work, they too glimpsed the divine. And Tihax, once a humble weaver, became a storyteller of the gods, his tapestry a testament to the day he soared with Kukulkan and saw the world through the eyes of a god.

[CHAPTER 36] — MAM

In the heart of the ancient city of Kaminaljuyú, where the great pyramids stood as silent witnesses to the passage of time, there lived a noble named Hunacel. His lineage was as old as the stones upon which the city was built, and his influence reached across the highlands and valleys that cradled his homeland. Yet, for all his power and wealth, Hunacel was troubled, for the earth beneath Kaminaljuyú had begun to tremble, whispers of discontent from the very heart of the world.

The people of Kaminaljuyú spoke in hushed tones of Mam, the god of earthquakes, a deity whose anger could split the earth and whose favor could ensure stability and prosperity. It was said that Mam resided deep within the mountains, where the roots of the earth drank from the primordial waters, and that he alone could command the land to quake or to rest.

Determined to protect his city and its people, Hunacel resolved to seek out Mam, to offer him tribute and plead for his mercy. With a retinue of his most trusted warriors and shamans, Hunacel embarked on a journey into the mountains, where the veil between the mortal world and the realm of the gods was thinnest.

For days they traveled, ascending through clouds and forests, until they reached a cave, its entrance a gaping maw in the mountainside, from which a cold, ancient breath emanated. It was here, the shamans whispered, that one could speak with Mam, if one dared.

Hunacel stepped forward, alone, and entered the cave. Inside, the air was thick with the weight of eons, and the stone beneath his feet vibrated with a power that spoke of the deep, restless heart of the earth. As his eyes adjusted to the dim light, Hunacel beheld Mam, not as a fearsome beast, but as an old man, his skin as rugged and weathered as the mountains themselves, his eyes deep pools of darkness from which no light escaped.

"Why have you come, noble of Kaminaljuyú?" Mam's voice was the rumble of distant thunder, the sound of the earth shifting far below.

Hunacel bowed, his heart heavy with the responsibility of his quest. "Great Mam, I come to beg your mercy. The earth trembles, and my people fear for their lives. What tribute can I offer to appease your anger and protect Kaminaljuyú?"

Mam's deep voice resonated once more through the cavern, "Balché to quench my thirst and ten virgins, including your own daughter, to be offered in sacrifice."

Hunacel, saddened at the god's request, nodded in acceptance. "It shall be done, Great Mam. We will prepare the balché with reverence, and the virgins, the most beautiful of our lands, will be offered to honor you, seeking your protection and benevolence."

Returning to Kaminaljuyú, Hunacel immediately set about organizing the offerings. The finest balché was brewed, a task given to the most skilled makers, who infused the drink with honey and roots, imbuing it with the richness of the earth. Meanwhile, ten of the most beautiful virgins in Kaminaljuyú, including Hunacel's own daughter, were selected for the sacrifice.

On the day of the offering, the people of Kaminaljuyú gathered at the foot of the nearest mountain, a place believed to be closest to Mam's domain. The air was filled with the scent of burning copal, purifying the space for the ritual. Hunacel, leading the ceremony, raised the jug of balché towards the sky, his voice steady as he invoked Mam's name, "Great Mam, accept this offering, may it quench your thirst and soothe your anger."

As the balché was poured onto the earth, a symbolic gesture of feeding the land, the virgins were offered one by one, their sacrifice made with respect and gratitude for the life they had given. The shamans chanted prayers, asking for Mam's mercy, for the earth to be gentle, and for the protection of Kaminaljuyú.

In the days that followed, the tremors that had once threatened the city's peace subsided. The people of Kaminaljuyú breathed easier, their faith in Mam's power and in the rituals of their ancestors reaffirmed.

Hunacel's leadership through this time of uncertainty strengthened the bonds within the community, reminding them of the importance of unity and respect for the forces that shaped their world. The ritual of the balché and the virgin sacrifices became an annual event, not just to appease Mam but as a celebration of their enduring relationship with the earth and its guardian deities.

[CHAPTER 37] — NACON

Amidst the dense jungles that cloak the land between Tikal and Calakmul, two great Mayan cities locked in an age-old rivalry, the air was thick with anticipation of war. It was here that a warrior, Yaxkin, prepared to fulfill his destiny under the watchful gaze of Nacon, the god of war. Yaxkin, whose name meant "New Sun," was renowned for his prowess in battle, his name whispered with reverence and fear among his people.

The conflict between Tikal and Calakmul had simmered for generations, a relentless pursuit of dominance that had claimed countless lives. War and combat played significant roles in Mayan society, not only for territorial expansion and control but also for capturing prisoners for tribute and ritual sacrifice, which were crucial elements in Mayan religious practices. This time, the dispute centered on control of fertile lands and access to precious resources. Both cities invoked Nacon, seeking his favor in the impending clash, offering sacrifices of jaguar blood and the hearts of captured enemies to stoke the god's thirst for conflict.

As dawn broke on the day of battle, Yaxkin stood before the imposing visage of Nacon, carved into a massive stone at the edge of the jungle. The air vibrated with the chants of priests, their voices rising in a plea for victory. Yaxkin, his body painted with symbols of power and protection, offered his own blood to Nacon, slicing the palm of his hand with an obsidian blade. "Great Nacon, guide my hand in battle, let my enemies falter before your might," he intoned, his voice steady and resolute.

The god of war, pleased with the fervor and dedication of his followers, whispered promises of glory and conquest into the hearts of the warriors. "Let the blood spilled this day nourish the earth and elevate your spirits to the heavens," Nacon's voice thundered, a sound only those chosen by fate could hear.

As the two armies clashed, the jungle itself seemed to recoil from the brutality of the conflict. Yaxkin moved through the ranks of his enemies with lethal grace, each strike guided by the hand of Nacon. The clash of obsidian on bone, the cries of the fallen, and the roar of victory and defeat melded into a symphony of chaos and valor.

The battle raged from sunrise to sunset, the ground soaked with the blood of the warriors. Yaxkin, though wounded, stood tall among the survivors, his spirit unbroken. In the aftermath, as the survivors tended to their wounds and mourned their dead, Yaxkin returned to the visage of Nacon.

"Great Nacon, your thirst for war has been quenched, but at what cost?" Yaxkin asked, his voice heavy with the toll of victory. The god of war, ever insatiable, replied, "The cycle of conflict is unending, Yaxkin. Today you have emerged victorious, but the seeds of future battles have been sown. Remember, it is through strife that strength is forged, and through sacrifice that power is gained."

Yaxkin, reflecting on Nacon's words, understood the dual nature of war — it was both destroyer and creator, ending lives while forging legends. As he departed from the bloodied battlefield, Yaxkin carried with him the weight of his actions and the knowledge that his destiny was forever intertwined with the will of the gods.

[CHAPTER 38] — PAWAHTUN

In the verdant heart of a world suspended between the veils of the seen and unseen, where the whispers of the ancient forest blend with the breath of the cosmos, there lived a feather worker named Mayel. Her art was not merely a craft but a communion with the divine, for she wove the essence of the skies into her creations, especially those from the resplendent quetzals, birds sacred to her people.

Mayel's gift was rare, a harmony of skill and spirit, allowing her to capture the iridescence of dawn and the mystery of twilight within the delicate embrace of feathers. Yet, as the seasons turned, her soul yearned for a deeper connection, a sign from the gods to guide her hand to even greater works.

It was during the zenith of the summer solstice, when the veil between worlds thins, that the Pawahtun, four guardians of the cosmic balance and patrons of scribes and artists, turned their gaze upon Mayel. They saw in her not just a feather worker but a vessel for their wisdom, a bridge between the earth and the divine.

That night, as Mayel sat beneath the canopy of stars, her hands idle and her heart open, the Pawahtun descended. They appeared not as fearsome deities but as ancient sages, their forms shimmering with the light of distant stars, each bearing the weight of the sky with a grace that belied their age.

"Mayel," they spoke, their voices a symphony of the winds, "your art has pleased us, for through your hands, the beauty of the heavens is reflected upon the earth. But true creation is not the work of hands alone; it is the song of the soul in harmony with the universe."

With these words, the Pawahtun bestowed upon Mayel a vision, a dance of colors and light where the boundaries between sky and earth blurred. She saw the quetzals not just as birds but as living fragments of the sky, their feathers a gift from the heavens to connect the mortal realm with the eternal.

Moved by the vision, Mayel's work transformed. Her fingers moved with newfound purpose, weaving not just feathers but the essence of wind, the warmth of the sun, and the mystery of the twilight into her creations. Each piece became a talisman, a beacon of the sacred balance the Pawahtun guarded.

As word of her extraordinary creations spread, people from distant lands came, seeking the magic imbued within her work. Mayel's art became a medium through which the whispers of the Pawahtun reached the hearts of all who beheld it, reminding them of the delicate dance of balance, of the unity between the heavens and the earth.

Mayel, now revered as a conduit of the divine, continued her work with humility and joy, ever grateful to the Pawahtun for their gift. In her legacy, the sacred bond between humanity and the cosmos was forever enshrined, a testament to the power of art to transcend the mundane and touch the divine.

And so, through the hands of a humble feather worker, the majesty of the Pawahtun was woven into the tapestry of the world, a reminder of the beauty and balance that sustains all life, seen and unseen.

[CHAPTER 39] — TOHIL

Under the cloak of a moonless night, in the shadowed lands of the K'iche' Maya, a chill ran through the village of Q'umarkaj. Within this realm of whispered legends and revered traditions, the presence of Tohil, the fire god and guardian of warmth and light, was a beacon to those who sought his favor and feared his wrath.

In this village lived a young man named Aapo, whose heart was as brave as it was restless. Aapo had heard the elders speak of Tohil, how the god's flames could either nurture life or summon destruction. It was said that Tohil's favor could ensure victory in battle, prosperity in trade, and warmth through the coldest of nights. Yet, his anger could scorch the earth, leaving only ashes in its wake.

Driven by a desire to protect his people from an encroaching cold that threatened their crops and their very survival, Aapo embarked on a quest to seek out Tohil's sacred temple, hidden deep within the mountains where eternal flames danced against the stone. The journey was perilous, filled with trials that tested Aapo's courage and resolve. But his determination was fueled by the love for his people and the hope that Tohil's divine fire would save them.

Upon reaching the temple, Aapo found himself standing before Tohil, whose form was as mesmerizing as the flames he controlled. Tohil's eyes burned with an intensity that pierced the darkness, his voice echoing like the crackle of fire in the still night.

"Why do you seek me, mortal?" Tohil's question was both an invitation and a challenge.

Aapo bowed, his voice steady despite the awe that filled him. "Great Tohil, I come to ask for your blessing. My people suffer in the cold, and I fear for their lives. Grant us your warmth, so we may survive the winter."

Tohil regarded Aapo, the flames around him flickering as if contemplating the young man's plea. "Your request is not light, Aapo. The fire I wield is a force both sacred and dangerous. It demands respect and sacrifice. What would you offer in return for such a gift?"

Aapo knew the weight of his request and the price it carried. "I offer my service to you, Tohil. Let me be a vessel for your warmth, to carry your fire back to my people."

Tohil's gaze softened, the flames leaping higher as if in approval. "Brave Aapo, your selflessness has earned my favor. But remember, fire is a gift and a responsibility. It must be tended with care, lest it consume all in its path."

With those words, Tohil bestowed upon Aapo a spark of his divine fire, a flame that would never wane, to bring back to Q'umarkaj. Aapo returned to his village, hailed as a hero, the bearer of Tohil's blessing. Under his watchful eye, the fire was shared among the hearths of his people, warding off the cold and ensuring their survival.

Yet, Aapo never forgot Tohil's warning. He taught his people to respect the fire, to see it not just as a source of warmth, but as a sacred gift that required vigilance and respect. And so, through the generations, the people of Q'umarkaj thrived, their lives intertwined with the eternal flame of Tohil, a reminder of the fire god's power and the young man who dared to seek his favor.

[CHAPTER 40] — WAYEB

In the woven tapestry of time that blankets the Mayan realm, there exists a span of days cloaked in whispers and shadowed by unease. It is the Wayeb, a fleeting but potent period when the fabric of the cosmos thins, and the barriers between worlds soften. Within this interlude, nestled between the end of one cycle and the birth of another, the presence of Wayeb, the enigmatic deity of these five perilous days, looms large over the people of the ancient city of Copán.

Nimá, a scribe of esteemed wisdom and respect, had long pondered the mysteries of the Wayeb. Unlike his contemporaries, who viewed these days with fear and trepidation, Nimá saw them as a time of deep reflection and potential understanding—a gateway to the divine that, if navigated with care, could yield profound insights.

As the Wayeb approached, the city of Copán grew still, its vibrant life pausing as if holding its breath. Families retreated into the safety of their homes, drawing symbols of protection on their doorways and whispering prayers into the night. Yet, Nimá ventured out, guided by an insatiable thirst for knowledge and a desire to commune directly with Wayeb.

Under the cloak of darkness, with only the stars to light his path, Nimá made his way to a secluded cenote, a sacred well that the ancients believed served as a portal to the underworld. It was here, at the nexus of the earthly and the divine, that Nimá sought audience with Wayeb.

The air around the cenote vibrated with unseen energy, and Nimá felt the veil between the worlds thinning, a gossamer thread ready to be unraveled. He called out to Wayeb, his voice steady but filled with reverence. "O Wayeb, guardian of the transition, I stand before you seeking wisdom. Show me the truths hidden within the shadows of the Wayeb."

For a moment, there was silence, a stillness so profound it seemed the world itself had ceased its endless turn. Then, from the depths of the cenote, a figure emerged. Wayeb, in form both terrifying and majestic, stood before Nimá, the embodiment of the chaotic potential that defined the Wayeb period.

"Why do you seek me, mortal?" Wayeb's voice was the sound of a thousand whispers, a cacophony of all the fears and hopes that the Wayeb harbored.

Nimá met Wayeb's gaze, his heart fortified by a lifetime of searching for truth. "I seek understanding, O Wayeb. Teach me how to navigate the uncertainties of life, how to find balance in the chaos."

Wayeb regarded Nimá, a flicker of interest igniting in the deity's ancient eyes. "Bravery and wisdom are rare companions, yet you possess both. The Wayeb is a reminder that life is a tapestry of light and shadow, order and chaos. Embrace both, for one cannot exist without the other. Seek balance within yourself, and you will navigate the Wayeb—and all of life's uncertainties—with grace."

With those words, Wayeb vanished, leaving Nimá alone beside the cenote, the night once more silent around him. Yet, within Nimá's heart, a fire had been lit, a spark of understanding that would guide him through the Wayeb and beyond.

Nimá returned to Copán, his spirit enriched by the encounter. Though he shared his experience with few, those who listened sensed the truth in his words. In the cycles that followed, Nimá became a beacon of wisdom, teaching others to see the Wayeb not as a time of fear, but as an opportunity for growth and reflection.

And so, through Nimá's teachings, the people of Copán learned to embrace the Wayeb, finding within its shadows the flickering light of understanding and balance, forever guided by the enigmatic presence of Wayeb, the deity who walks between the worlds.

[CHAPTER 41] — VUCUB CAQUIX

In the verdant realms of the ancient Mayan lands, where the sky kisses the canopy of the endless forest, and the rivers whisper secrets of old, there thrived a creature of unmatched vanity and power. Vucub Caquix, the Seven Macaw, with feathers that shimmered like gold, dazzling, jewel-encrusted teeth, and eyes that glowed as bright as the morning star, roosted atop the tallest nance tree. He declared himself the sun, the moon, and the very light that pierced the darkness of the night.

Yet, his claims did not go unchallenged. From the shadows cast by the towering ceibas and amidst the chorus of the jungle, emerged two figures destined to confront the false luminary— Hunahpú and Xbalanque, the Hero Twins. Born of divine lineage and crafted by the very essence of creation, they were the embodiment of cunning, strength, and resolve.

The twins, having heard of the bird's boastful proclamations, devised a plan to humble him, to strip him of his pretentious glow and reveal his true nature to the world. With blowguns in hand, they set out at dawn, when the mist still clung to the earth, whispering of their impending deed.

As they approached Vucub Caquix's abode, Hunahpú aimed and released a dart from his blowgun. It soared, a silent promise of justice, and struck the magnificent bird, but only managed to injure his jaw. Enraged and in pain, Vucub Caquix swooped down upon the twins, a tempest of feathers and fury.

The battle that ensued was fierce, the jungle echoing with the clash of divine wills. The twins, agile and wise beyond their years, evaded the bird's assaults, weaving through the trees like spirits of the wind. "Your light is but a shadow upon the true brilliance of the sun and moon," Xbalanque taunted, his voice steady and resolute.

Realizing brute force would not subdue their foe, the twins resorted to guile. They sought the aid of two elderly gods, their grandparents, Ixmucané and Ixpiyacoc, who agreed to help in their quest. Together, they crafted a plan to remove the source of Vucub Caquix's pride—his bejeweled teeth and metallic eyes.

Under the magical guise of dentists, the twins offered to cure the bird's aching jaw, replacing his glittering teeth with white corn and plucking the precious metals from his eyes. Deprived of his false radiance, Vucub Caquix's strength waned, and he was finally humbled.

Defeated, the great bird fled into the shadows of the forest, his cries a testament to the twins' cunning and the folly of his arrogance. Yet, the tale of Vucub Caquix served as a warning to all who would listen: that the true light of the cosmos cannot be claimed by mere proclamation, and that humility precedes true greatness.

The Hero Twins, their mission fulfilled, returned to their people, heralded as protectors of the balance between light and darkness. They had not only vanquished a formidable foe but had also restored the natural order, ensuring that the true sun and moon could shine upon the world unchallenged, not knowing that they themselves would eventually be the true sun and moon.

[CHAPTER 42] — XAMAN EK

In the twilight of the ancient Mayan civilization, when the cities were alive with commerce and the roads whispered the stories of countless travelers, there lived a merchant named Iktan. Iktan was known throughout the lands for his trade in rare feathers, sourced from the deepest jungles and most remote corners of the Mayan realm. His journeys were legendary, often fraught with peril, as he navigated through dense forests and over rugged mountains to bring back the vibrant plumage of quetzals and macaws for the nobility and priests in the great city of Tikal. Yet, it was not just his bravery or the allure of his goods that set Iktan apart; it was his unwavering faith in Xaman Ek, the North Star god, who guided him through the darkest nights and most treacherous paths.

On one particular voyage, Iktan set out from Tikal, bound for the coastal city of Tulum, with a cargo of feathers that shimmered like the very stars under Xaman Ek's watchful gaze. These feathers were destined for the grand ceremonies that would honor the gods and ensure the prosperity of the Mayan people. As he embarked on his journey, Iktan offered prayers to Xaman Ek, seeking his protection and guidance, for the route was known to be laden with bandits and wild beasts, and the dense jungle could disorient even the most experienced traveler.

The first days of Iktan's journey were uneventful, as he followed the ancient sacbeob, the white roads that connected the Mayan cities like a web woven by the gods themselves. However, as he ventured deeper into the wilderness, a sudden storm descended upon him, turning day into night and the familiar path into a maze of shadows and uncertainty. It was then, in his darkest moment, that Iktan felt the presence of Xaman Ek, a comforting warmth amidst the cold rain and howling wind.

In a vision that pierced the tempest's fury, Xaman Ek appeared before Iktan, his form radiant and serene, a beacon of hope in the storm's wrath. "Fear not, Iktan," the god spoke, his voice the gentle hum of the cosmos. "For I have watched over your journeys, and I see the devotion in your heart. Follow my light, and you shall find your way."

Grasping the amulet of Xaman Ek he always wore, Iktan looked to the heavens and saw, through the breaks in the storm clouds, the unwavering light of the North

Star. With renewed resolve, he pressed onward, guided by the celestial light that pierced the darkness.

The storm raged on, but Iktan's path remained clear, as if the very jungle conspired to aid him in his quest. When bandits lay in wait, they found themselves blinded by sudden flashes of light, allowing Iktan to pass unharmed. When wild beasts prowled nearby, they were calmed by an unseen force, their growls fading into the night.

After many days and nights, Iktan emerged from the jungle's embrace, the gates of Tulum welcoming him like the arms of an old friend. His journey, blessed by Xaman Ek, was a testament to the power of faith and the protection of the gods.

The feathers Iktan brought to Tulum were more than mere adornments; they were symbols of the divine journey he had undertaken, a journey watched over by Xaman Ek. As he shared his tale with those who gathered to see his wares, the story of his voyage became a legend, a reminder of the guiding light that awaits all who seek it in the darkness.

[CHAPTER 43] — XBALANQUE AND HUNAHPÚ

Born of divine lineage, their father, Hun-Hunahpu, was a skilled ball player who met his end in the underworld of Xibalba, decapitated by the lords of the dead. Their mother, Ixquic, conceived them through a miraculous encounter with the severed head of Hun-Hunahpu. From their earliest days, the twins were destined to avenge their father's death, challenge the gods of the underworld, and restore balance to the cosmos.

Raised by their grandmother, Ixmucané, Xbalanque and Hunahpú grew up hidden from the malevolent gaze of the lords of Xibalba. Their childhood was marked by feats of extraordinary strength and intelligence, which they used to outwit their older half-brothers and transform them into the constellation Pleiades, thus beginning their journey of heroism.

Even as children, the twins showed an innate mastery of the ball game, an essential skill that would later prove crucial in their confrontation with the lords of Xibalba. Their prowess inevitably attracted the attention of the underworld deities, who saw in the twins the echo of their father's defiance and sought to put an end to their lineage once and for all.

Their father, Hun-Hunahpu, once a revered ball player, had met his demise at the hands of the treacherous lords of Xibalba. His defeat and subsequent death were not just personal tragedies but a dishonor to his name that resonated through the heavens and the earth. It was this stain upon their family's honor that spurred Xbalanque and Hunahpú, the hero twins, to venture into the very heart of darkness: Xibalba, the underworld.

Their journey was fraught with peril, a path that few had tread and even fewer had survived. Yet, with hearts bolstered by righteous fury and spirits guided by the divine, the twins descended into the abyss. The entrance to Xibalba was a deceptive one, a cavernous maw that swallowed light and hope alike. But the twins were undeterred, for their mission was one of retribution and restoration.

Their first trial awaited in the Dark House, a chamber void of all light, where darkness was not just an absence of light but a palpable entity that sought to smother all who entered. The lords of Xibalba, amused by their audacity, presented them with torches and cigars, instructing them to keep them alight throughout the night. It was a test designed for failure, for no mortal flame could survive the oppressive darkness of the Dark House.

But Xbalanque and Hunahpú were no ordinary mortals. With a cunning born of celestial lineage, they called upon the fireflies, those tiny bearers of light, and attached them to the ends of their torches and cigars. The fireflies' glow was indistinguishable from the flame the lords expected to see, and thus the twins fooled their would-be executioners, passing the first test with their ingenuity.

Their triumph in the Dark House, however, was but the prelude to a more daunting challenge: the Razor House. Within its walls, the air was thick with menace, the silence punctuated by the sinister whisper of blades. These were no ordinary knives but enchanted ones, gifted with malevolent life by the dark magics of Xibalba, eager to taste the blood of the living.

As the blades lunged and danced with lethal grace, Xbalanque and Hunahpú stood their ground. Understanding that brute force would avail them naught against such foes, they instead chose to parley with the knives. With words as sharp as the blades they faced, they spoke of the sanctity of life and the honor of their quest, appealing to the sliver of creation magic that gave the knives their deadly purpose.

The knives, never before addressed as equals by gods or mortals, were taken aback by the twins' audacity. Moved by their plea, they ceased their deadly ballet, allowing Xbalanque and Hunahpú to spend the night unharmed. The Razor House, like the Dark House before it, had been conquered not by strength of arms but by strength of spirit.

Emerging from the Razor House with their bodies and spirits unscathed and their resolve strengthened, Xbalanque and Hunahpú prepared to face the next trial laid out by the dark-hearted lords of Xibalba. The Cold House awaited them, its very name a whisper of dread. As they stepped into its icy embrace, the warmth of life seemed to drain from their bodies, replaced by the biting caress of frost. The air was so frigid it turned their breath to mist, and the ground beneath their feet crackled with the cold.

But the hero twins were not to be deterred by the chill that sought to claim them. Remembering the fireflies that had aided them in the Dark House, they called upon these small bearers of light once more. This time, the fireflies did not merely serve as a ruse; their gentle glow became a source of warmth, a beacon of hope in the oppressive cold. Clutching the fireflies and each other close, Xbalanque and Hunahpú found the strength to endure the night, their breath steady in the face of the cold that sought to silence them. By dawn, the Cold House had been conquered, not through brute force but through the enduring warmth of hope and ingenuity.

The trial of the Jaguar House was next, a challenge that promised not cold, but the heat of danger and the shadow of death. The doors of the Jaguar House swung open to reveal a darkness alive with the growl of hunger, the eyes of the jaguars gleaming like stars of malice. The lords of Xibalba watched with bated breath, anticipating the moment the great cats would leap and the twins would meet their end. But Xbalanque and Hunahpú, sons of a lineage both divine and cunning, had no intention of becoming prey.

They had collected the bones from their previous meals, remnants of their journey through Xibalba, and these they used as a diversion. Casting the bones before the jaguars, the twins watched as hunger turned the predators from hunters into scavengers, their attention captured by the promise of an easier meal. The jaguars feasted on bones, and the twins passed the night untouched, their cleverness turning potential executioners into unwitting guardians.

The Fire House loomed before them as the next crucible, its heart a blaze that danced with hungry flames. The twins were met with a heat that sought to consume not just flesh but spirit, a fire that roared with the arrogance of the undefeated. But Xbalanque and Hunahpú had walked through darkness, stilled the bite of frost, and silenced the hunger of beasts. Fire, no matter how fierce, was but another puzzle to be solved.

With careful steps and keen observation, they navigated the labyrinth of flames, using their knowledge of the wind and the ways of fire to find the paths where the flames burned less fiercely. They moved with the grace of those who understood the essence of the elements, their respect for the fire's power guiding them safely through its domain.

As the emerged from the Fire House, the twins were unburned, standing amidst the coals as testament to their mastery over the trials set before them. The lords of Xibalba, watching in disbelief, were forced to acknowledge the prowess and resilience of Xbalanque and Hunahpú. Yet, the underworld was deep and dark, its secrets many, and the twins knew their journey was far from over

The Bat House awaited next, its ominous silhouette a harbinger of dread. Within, the air was thick with the flutter of countless wings, the silence shattered by the piercing screeches of deadly bats, servants to the sinister bat god, Camazotz.

The twins, ever resourceful, sought refuge within their blowguns, which they enlarged with magic, a clever ploy to shield themselves from the aerial predators. The night stretched on, a tense vigil of darkness and danger. As dawn approached, Hunahpú, driven by a momentary lapse of caution, peered out to greet the morning light. It was then that Camazotz struck, a swift and terrible blow that decapitated Hunahpú, plunging Xbalanque into despair.

Yet, despair soon gave way to determination. Xbalanque, his heart set on undoing this grave injustice, devised a bold plan. With meticulous care, he fashioned a squash into the likeness of Hunahpú's head, a decoy to deceive their adversaries. This act of deception was but the first step in a grander scheme to reclaim his brother's head and restore his life.

The stage was set for the ultimate confrontation: the ball game against the lords of Xibalba. The stakes were higher than ever, the game charged with the weight of vengeance and redemption. During the ball game, the twins displayed remarkable teamwork and cunning. Xbalanque, ever the strategist, took the forefront in the game, compensating for his brother's temporary incapacitation, while Hunahpu, despite his headless condition, supported as best as he could under the magical guise that made the squash head seem alive. The lords of Xibalba, none the wiser, played against the twins, fully believing they were competing against both in their entirety.

Xbalanque also used magic to use a ball that was, in reality, a wasp's nest. Xbalanque's agility, intelligence, and divine backing allowed them to outmaneuver the lords at every turn. In the end, when the game was won, the deception was revealed. The twins used this moment not only to highlight the folly and hubris of the lords of Xibalba but also to reclaim Hunahpú's head. The squash, having served its purpose, was discarded, and Hunahpu was fully restored, whole once again, through the same divine magic that had allowed them to deceive the underworld's rulers.

Emboldened by their victory, the twins embarked on a campaign to dismantle the power of the Xibalban lords. They unleashed their divine might, setting ablaze the homes of their oppressors, shattering the chains of fear that had long bound the denizens of Xibalba. With each feat, they diminished the lords' dominion, their actions a declaration of liberation for all who suffered under the yoke of the underworld.

In the aftermath of their rebellion, the twins sought to recover their father's remains, a final act of filial piety and respect. Though they could not fully resurrect Hun-Hunahpu, their efforts were not in vain. The saga of their father, from his demise to this moment of reverence, was a narrative arc that spanned the heavens and the earth, a story of fall and redemption, of death and the undying hope for renewal.

The culmination of their journey was not merely the defeat of the Xibalban lords or the avenging of their father and uncle. Recognizing their divine heritage and the balance they had restored, the gods elevated Xbalanque and Hunahpú to the heavens. Xbalanque became the moon, casting a soothing, reflective light across the night sky, while Hunahpú transformed into the sun, bringing warmth and illumination to the world.

Their legacy, immortalized in the sky above, was a testament to their heroism, a reminder of the indomitable spirit of those who dare to challenge the darkness. In their ascent, Xbalanque and Hunahpú transcended their mortal origins, becoming enduring symbols of unity, hope, resilience, and the eternal quest for justice and harmony in the cosmos.

[CHAPTER 44] — YALUK

In the heart of the ancient city of Yaxchilán, where the Usumacinta River bends and whispers ancient tales, there lived a painter named Zacai. His hands were gifted in the art of capturing the essence of life, the spirits of the gods, and the mysteries of the cosmos on the walls of the grand temples and palaces. It was said that Zacai could speak to the stones, and in return, they revealed to him the colors of the universe.

One season, when the rains were scarce, and the land thirsted for the touch of Chaac, the rain god, Zacai embarked on a quest to create his most ambitious work yet. He sought to paint a mural that would honor Yaluk, the deity of lightning and thunder, whose fierce energy ignited the skies and whose power was both feared and revered.

As Zacai pondered upon the mural, he realized that to truly capture Yaluk's essence, he needed to witness the god's power firsthand. He prayed to Yaluk, offering copal incense and blue cacao beans, a rare delicacy known to please the gods. Zacai's heart was pure, his intentions noble, to bring hope and inspire awe among his people during the dry spell.

One night, as the stars watched in silent anticipation, Zacai's prayers were answered. The air around him crackled with electricity, and the sky darkened as if night had decided to reclaim the day. Then, with a roar that shook the earth and silenced the creatures of the forest, Yaluk appeared before Zacai in a brilliant flash of light.

Yaluk, manifesting not as a fearsome force but in the form of a majestic macaw with feathers that shimmered like flames, spoke to Zacai. "Why do you summon me, mortal? What is it that you seek in the tempest?"

Zacai, his heart pounding yet filled with a sense of calm bestowed by the divine presence, replied, "Great Yaluk, I seek to honor you through my art, to capture your might and beauty so that future generations may know of your power and the balance you bring to the world. But to do so, I must understand the essence of your lightning and fire."

Yaluk regarded Zacai for a moment, the air around them charged with an unseen energy. Then, with a voice that rumbled like distant thunder yet carried the warmth of a gentle flame, Yaluk agreed. "Very well, Zacai. Witness my power and understand the heart of the storm."

That night, Yaluk took Zacai on a journey through the skies, where the painter witnessed the birth of lightning, the dance of thunder, and the delicate balance between destruction and renewal. Zacai saw the way lightning nourished the earth, sparking life in its wake, and how fire cleared the old to make way for new growth.

With each flash of light, each peal of thunder, Zacai's vision for the mural took shape. He saw the colors of the storm, the hues of fire and electricity, and the gentle touch of rain that followed. Yaluk taught him that true power lay not in fear and destruction but in the ability to inspire growth, change, and awe.

Upon returning to Yaxchilán, Zacai set to work, his brushes and paints guided by the divine experience. The mural he created was unlike any seen before, a vivid portrayal of Yaluk's dual nature as both destroyer and nurturer. It depicted the macaw god amidst a storm, with lightning in his beak and fire in his wings, surrounded by the vibrant life that flourished after the rain.

The people of Yaxchilán were captivated by Zacai's mural, and in the seasons that followed, the rains returned, nurturing the land once more. Zacai's masterpiece stood as a testament to the power of faith, the beauty of the natural world, and the profound connection between the divine and the creative spirit of humanity.

[CHAPTER 45] — YUM KAAX

In the dense underbrush of the jungle that enshrouds Aguateca, where the canopy's embrace shields the secrets of the ancient world, a young hunter named Kan moved with silent precision. His skill with the bow was unmatched, his steps silent on the forest floor, yet within him stirred a hunger for a conquest that would etch his name into the annals of legend.

One humid afternoon, as the jungle teemed with the cacophony of life, Kan's eyes settled on a magnificent jaguar, its coat a tapestry of shadows and light. The hunter, driven by the thrill of the chase and the glory of the kill, nocked an arrow to his bow, the beast unaware of its peril. But as Kan drew back his bowstring, tension singing in the air between predator and prey, the jungle itself seemed to hold its breath.

It was then that Yum Kaax appeared, not as a whisper of wind or a shadow flickering at the edge of sight, but as a towering presence, the very essence of the jungle made manifest. The deity stood before Kan, an ethereal figure clad in the verdant hues of the forest, his eyes reflecting the depths of nature's wisdom.

"Why do you raise your weapon against my children, hunter?" Yum Kaax's voice was the rustle of leaves, the rumble of distant thunder, commanding yet not without warmth. "Is it not enough to take from the forest what you need, that you seek to claim lives for the sake of pride?"

Kan, struck by the gravity of the god's words, lowered his bow, shame and realization dawning upon him. The jaguar, sensing the shift in the air, slipped away, a silent shadow once more. "Great Yum Kaax," Kan began, his voice barely a whisper, "I sought only to prove my worth, to become the greatest hunter known to my people. I now see the folly of my ways. In my quest for glory, I have forgotten the sacred balance that sustains us all."

Yum Kaax nodded, the forest around them alive with unseen energies. "To hunt is to partake in the cycle of life and death," the deity spoke, "but to do so with respect and understanding is to honor that cycle. Remember, hunter, that each creature plays a role in the fabric of the forest. Protect that balance, as I do, and you shall find true honor."

In that moment, Kan's purpose was transformed. He vowed to become a guardian of the forest, to hunt only in necessity and to defend the wilds against those who would do it harm. His legend grew, not from the trophies of his hunts, but from his dedication to preserving the harmony of the jungle.

Years passed, and Kan's story became a beacon for his people, a testament to the power of change and the importance of living in harmony with the natural world. And though he walked the paths of the forest alone, he was never truly alone, for Yum Kaax watched over him, a constant presence guiding him in his new role as protector of the jungle.

[CHAPTER 46] — YUMIL KAXOB

In the heart of the Mayan lands, within the thriving city of Edzna, there lived a diligent farmer named Pachac. For generations, his family had toiled over the same fields, coaxing maize from the earth with the sweat of their brows. Yet, despite their efforts, the once fertile land began to yield less each season. The problem was not drought, the rain was coming as it always had, but the consequence of years of monoculture that depleted the soil of its nutrients.

Pachac was on the brink of despair when Yumil Kaxob, the revered god of maize, appeared before him in a vision. The deity's presence was as commanding as the sun, and his voice, though gentle, carried the weight of ages.

"Your fields suffer, not from the lack of rain, but from the absence of understanding," Yumil Kaxob began, his gaze sweeping across the barren fields. "The soil is tired, drained of life by the constant demand of a single crop. You must embrace the wisdom of the 'Three Sisters'."

Intrigued, Pachac listened intently as Yumil Kaxob detailed the practice of the Milpa system. "Plant maize, beans, and squash together," the god instructed. "These three sisters will support and nourish each other and the earth."

He explained how the maize would provide a natural trellis for the beans to climb, ensuring they could bask in the sun's embrace. "The beans," he continued, "are more than climbers. They commune with the air, capturing nitrogen and enriching the soil, a gift to all who share this space."

Yumil Kaxob then spoke of the squash, its broad leaves a living mulch that cooled the earth, conserving moisture and thwarting the advance of weeds. "Together, these sisters weave a bond stronger than their roots, creating a harmony that sustains the circle of life."

Pachac, heartened by the god's wisdom, implemented the Milpa system. He planted the three sisters together, marveling at how they flourished in unison, each contributing to the health of the others and the land itself. As the seasons turned, his fields, once on the brink of failure, became a testament to balance and abundance.

The crops grew strong and bountiful, and Pachac's harvests multiplied. The community, witnessing the transformation of Pachac's fields, soon adopted the Milpa system too, heralding a new era of prosperity for Edzna.

Through Yumil Kaxob's guidance, Pachac learned that true wealth lies not only in the quantity of the harvest, but also in the health of the earth that sustains it. The Milpa system was more than an agricultural technique; it was a philosophy of life, a reminder of the interconnectedness of all things and the importance of giving back as much as we take.

Pachac's fields became a living legacy of Yumil Kaxob's visitation, a symbol of harmony between the earth and its caretakers. And in every ear of maize, in every bean vine, and in the shade of every squash leaf, the spirit of the Milpa whispered the ancient truths of balance, respect, and renewal.

[CHAPTER 47] — ZIPACNA

In the shadowed valleys near Iximché, where the mist weaves through the dense canopy and the mountains stretch towards the heavens, there lived a being of formidable strength and ancient lineage. Zipacna, with the body of a caiman and the might to shift the very bones of the earth, roamed these lands, claiming the creation of its towering peaks as his deed. His presence was a constant reminder of the raw power that lay beneath the surface, a power that both awed and frightened the inhabitants of the nearby city.

Zipacna's claims of crafting the mountains upon which Iximché stood were met with mixed feelings among its people. While some marveled at his extraordinary abilities, others whispered of his arrogance and the danger it posed. It was this mixture of fear and resentment that led the 400 boys, young men of the city, to devise a plan to rid their world of Zipacna's looming threat.

Under the guise of seeking his assistance in raising a new mountain, a monument to their city's greatness, they approached Zipacna. With cunning words, they flattered his ego and enticed him with promises of legacy and honor. Zipacna, ever proud of his strength, agreed, and together they ventured to a chosen site where the new mountain would stand.

The boys guided Zipacna to a vast pit they had prepared, explaining that its creation was the first step in their grand design. Zipacna, intrigued by the project, descended into the pit to begin his work. Unbeknownst to him, the boys had other intentions. As he delved deeper, crafting the foundation of what he believed would be his greatest creation yet, the boys rolled massive stones towards the pit, intending to crush him beneath its weight.

But Zipacna was no ordinary being. His connection to the earth, to the very essence of creation, granted him a perception beyond that of mortals. Sensing the deceit, he carved a secret tunnel from the pit's depths, escaping the boys' trap. He lay in wait, silent as the stone, as the boys, believing their plan a success, came to witness the outcome of their treachery.

As they peered into the pit, Zipacna emerged with the fury of a tempest, his betrayal fueling a rage that knew no bounds. One by one, he exacted his vengeance upon the 400 boys, their numbers offering no advantage against his might. In the aftermath, the earth itself seemed to mourn, the skies darkening and the winds whispering tales of sorrow and regret.

The tale of Zipacna and the 400 boys passed into legend, a stark reminder of the complex weave of admiration and envy, of the power inherent in the land and those who claim dominion over its mysteries. Zipacna, though avenged, retreated deeper into the embrace of the mountains he claimed as his own, his legacy a cautionary tale that echoed through the generations.

[CHAPTER 48] — ZOTZ

In the dense foliage that enshrouded Uaxactún, where the canopy whispered secrets of ages past and the earth teemed with the untold mysteries of the Maya, there lived a potter named Ahana. Her hands, skilled in the ancient craft, shaped the very soul of the earth into vessels that told stories of her people's glory, their dreams, and their fears. Yet, Ahana sought something more, a clay so rare, it was said to be blessed by the gods themselves, hidden in the heart of a cave guarded by Zotz, the bat god.

Legends spoke of Zotz's realm, a cavernous abyss where day never broke, and the guardians of the night reigned supreme. It was a place of power, of creation and destruction, where the very essence of life could be reforged in the shadows. Driven by a vision that visited her in dreams, Ahana ventured into the depths of the jungle, her heart set on discovering the sacred clay that would imbue her creations with the essence of the divine.

As she approached the cave's maw, the air grew thick, the whispers of the forest falling silent before the echo of wings. The entrance was veiled in darkness, a passage to a world untouched by the sun's embrace. Drawing a deep breath, Ahana stepped into the domain of Zotz, her torch casting a feeble light against the pressing darkness.

The sound of countless wings stirred in the shadows, a living tapestry woven from the night itself. Ahana pressed forward, her resolve unwavering, until the narrow passage opened into a vast chamber. There, amidst the stalactites that adorned the ceiling like ancient chandeliers, hung Zotz, a deity of immense presence, his eyes gleaming with the light of unnumbered stars.

"Why does a child of the sun dare to tread in my realm?" Zotz's voice filled the chamber, a sound that was both a growl and a whisper.

Ahana, her heart pounding in her chest, found the courage to speak. "Great Zotz, I come in search of the sacred clay, to craft vessels that honor the gods and my people. I seek your blessing, not to defy your domain."

Zotz regarded her, his gaze piercing the veil of mortality. "You seek the clay that births life from darkness, a gift from the heart of the earth. What tribute do you offer for this boon?"

Ahana knelt, presenting a vessel she had crafted, its surface a canvas of her dreams. "I offer this, my art, a testament to the journey of my soul. May it find favor in your eyes."

The god of bats descended, his form shifting, until he stood before Ahana, a being of majesty and terror. He examined the vessel, his touch a whisper against its surface. "Your offering is accepted, child of the sun. The clay you seek lies beyond, bathed in the eternal night. Take what you need, but remember, all gifts bear the weight of their cost."

Guided by Zotz's decree, Ahana found the sacred clay, its touch cool and alive against her skin. She shaped it with reverence, each vessel a prayer made manifest. And when she emerged from the cave, the first light of dawn greeted her, a world reborn in the glow of morning.

Ahana's pottery transcended mere function to become a canvas for the mystical interplay between the earthly and the divine. Each piece she crafted was imbued with the essence of Zotz, the guardian of the night and the mysterious depths from which she had drawn the sacred clay. Her hands, guided by a newfound reverence for the bat god and the secrets he protected, shaped vessels that were not only containers but also storytellers, whispering tales of the unseen world to those who would listen.

One of her most striking creations was a large ceremonial urn, its surface a dark canvas on which she depicted the flight of Zotz through the night sky. The bat god was rendered in exquisite detail, his wings outstretched, embracing the moon's silver glow. Around him, smaller bats danced in an aerial ballet, their forms etched with such precision that they seemed to flutter with life at the urn's slightest movement.

Another notable piece was a series of bowls, each bearing the motif of the bat's eyes. Ahana crafted these eyes with layers of glaze that captured the depth and mystery of Zotz's gaze. In the flicker of firelight, the eyes appeared to open and close, a mesmerizing effect that reminded the viewer of the god's ever-watchful presence.

Ahana also created a set of drinking vessels, each designed to represent the cave that had been Zotz's domain. The exteriors of these cups were textured to mimic the rough stone of cave walls, while the interiors were smooth and gleaming, symbolizing the sacred space within. On each cup, a small figure of Zotz hung upside down, a guardian overseeing the sacred act of drinking.

Perhaps the most ambitious of her works was a large platter, intended for use in communal ceremonies. The platter's rim was adorned with a frieze of bats in flight, each one carrying a symbol of the Mayan cosmos — stars, moons, and the planets known to the ancient astronomers. At the platter's center, Ahana depicted Zotz himself, not as a fearsome deity, but in a protective pose, wings enveloping the symbols of life: maize, beans, and squash. This piece spoke of Zotz's dual nature as both a destroyer and a protector, a god who held the power of creation within the shadows.

Through these creations, Ahana did more than honor a god; she wove a narrative of balance, of the symbiotic relationship between light and darkness, life and death. Her pottery became highly sought after, not just for its beauty and craftsmanship, but for its ability to connect the mundane with the mystical, the human with the divine.

In every piece, Ahana left a part of her journey, a testament to her encounter with Zotz and the transformative power of facing one's fears to discover the beauty hidden in the darkness. Her legacy was one of artistic brilliance and spiritual insight, a bridge between worlds that, through her art, allowed others to glimpse the profound mysteries she had encountered in the heart of the earth, under the watchful eyes of the bat god.

ABOUT THE AUTHOR

Samuel DenHartog's journey as a storyteller ventures into the mystical realms of ancient civilizations with his latest endeavor, "Tales from the Mayan Divine." Renowned for his ability to traverse genres with ease and depth, Samuel brings his signature passion and insight to explore the rich tapestry of Mayan mythology. Through his vivid storytelling, readers are transported to a world where gods and humans intertwine, revealing the complexities and wonders of a culture that has fascinated scholars and dreamers alike.

With each narrative, Samuel crafts a bridge between the past and the present, illuminating the enduring wisdom and spiritual vitality of the Mayan people. His work reflects an unyielding quest for the universal truths hidden within age-old tales, demonstrating his profound respect for the cultural heritage that continues to shape our understanding of the world. As a polymath with an insatiable thirst for knowledge, Samuel's writings are gateways to understanding the human spirit and its connection to the divine. "Tales from the Mayan Divine" is an invitation to embark on a journey through the heart of the Mayan civilization, to uncover the legends that have pulsed through the heart of the jungle and stood the test of time, celebrating the legacy of Mayan mythology.

Printed in Great Britain
by Amazon

acbcd44f-5986-4188-8ed4-ef124e98402dR01